LADY IN LINGERIE

LINGERIE #3

PENELOPE SKY

Hartwick Publishing

Lady in Lingerie

Copyright © 2018 by Penelope Sky

All rights reserved.

No part of this book may be reproduced in any form or by any electronic or mechanical means, including information storage and retrieval systems, without written permission from the author, except for the use of brief quotations in a book review.

CONTENTS

1. Conway	1
2. Sapphire	11
3. Conway	43
4. Sapphire	73
5. Conway	109
6. Sapphire	145
7. Conway	167
8. Sapphire	223
9. Conway	235
10. Sapphire	265
11. Conway	273
12. Sapphire	293
Also by Penelope Sky	313

1
CONWAY

Carter poured himself a glass of scotch and made himself comfortable on the sofa in my office. Darkness had settled a long time ago. I had dinner with Muse on the terrace, and then she went to bed. Carter stopped by shortly afterward, and now we were hidden away in my office.

He lit his cigar and let the smoke rise from his mouth toward the ceiling. "Your family loves Muse more than you do."

My eyes darted to his face, the lethal daggers practically bursting from my irises.

Carter chuckled before he took another puff of his cigar. "Sorry. Sapphire."

No one called her Muse but me. "Yes, I'm aware."

"Honestly, I like her more than you, too."

"Jump on the bandwagon," I said with indifference. "You've always been the type."

"I make my own way in life. If not, I wouldn't be a self-made billionaire." He switched off between enjoying his scotch and his cigar.

My office always smelled like cigars for days afterward, but I didn't mind because I liked the smell. None of my pieces were in here, so I didn't have to worry about ruining the fabric with the carcinogen.

"So, is she still your prisoner or what?" he asked. "Because it seems like you actually like the woman."

I did like her—a little too much. "I don't know what the fuck is going on, man."

He set his cigar on the ashtray and stared at me with his arms resting on his thighs. "Meaning?"

"My father asked when I was going to ask her to marry me."

Carter stopped making jokes when he knew I was being dead serious. He must have sensed the conflict inside my soul. We grew up together, so we understood each other on an innate level other people couldn't understand. It reminded me of my connection with Muse, but in a different way. "And what did you say?"

"That I wasn't ready for that kind of commitment. But my father never asks me stuff like that. And then he told me I shouldn't drag my feet because women like Sapphire are rare. He said she has spunk."

"She does have spunk," he said in agreement.

"But she also has class and beauty. She's got it all." I drank from my glass, letting the ice cubes hit my lips when the glass turned empty. "Then my mother told me how proud she was... That I'd become a man she was proud of. Made me fucking sick to my stomach."

"That's the kind of affection every son wants to hear from his parents."

"But I don't deserve it." I slammed my empty glass on the table, nearly shattering it. "I hate lying to my parents. Makes me feel like shit."

Carter shifted his gaze down to his glass. "Then what are you going to do?"

"I don't fucking know. But now I hate myself. I hate the way I collected Sapphire like a piece of property rather than a person. I hate the way I've treated her. Hate the things I said to her. My family adores her, and somehow, that makes me feel worse. If they knew what I did, my parents would never forgive me. Vanessa would never look at me the same."

"Then don't let them find out."

I turned my gaze out the window, my fingers resting against my temple. "Secrets always come out...in time."

"Then what choice do you have?" He picked up his

cigar again and breathed in the smoke. "You could let her go. You'd be out a hundred million dollars, but then you wouldn't be lying anymore. It could clear your conscience."

That was my best option, but I didn't like it. "I don't want to let her go..." I wanted her to stay with me. I wanted her in my bed every night. I needed her to inspire me, to pull the best work out of me. What would I be without her? I needed her. "And she wouldn't be safe if I did. If Knuckles ever figured it out, he would probably come after her."

"That's her problem, not yours."

My heart thudded harder in my chest. The idea of anyone stripping her naked and using her against her will made me sick. She deserved to be treated with respect, to live her life freely without fear of rape and torture. The only place she would ever be safe was by my side. I was the only one powerful enough to keep the demons away. "If something ever happened to her, I would die."

Carter watched me as he let the smoke out through his nostrils. He had the same hard features as mine, and I felt like I was looking at a brother instead of a cousin. "You care about this woman."

I wasn't going to deny it anymore. "Deeply."

"Then let it be. She's safe here with you and seems happy."

"Doesn't right my wrongs. Doesn't clear my head."

"Then what other option do you have?"

I didn't have any options. I wanted to make this right, but I didn't know how. I couldn't go back in time and erase my mistakes. I couldn't go back and not demand sex from her. I couldn't take back all the hurtful things I said, the disrespectful way I treated her. I couldn't give her back her virginity when I took it so ruthlessly. I couldn't change the foundation of our relationship. "I don't know…"

"You could set her free," Carter said. "And let her decide what she wants."

But what if she made the wrong decision? What if she left me? I'd be devastated. "And if she leaves?"

He shrugged. "Don't give her a reason to leave. Give her a reason to stay. Or as many reasons as she needs."

NICOLE MADE ALL THE NECESSARY ARRANGEMENTS FOR me, and by the end of the afternoon, I had successfully wired the funds to the American authorities and paid back all the money that Muse owed. She owed immense property taxes that were never paid, in addition to the loan she defaulted on. She also had student loans for a degree she never finished. Once the money was transferred, Muse was officially cleared.

She didn't owe anything.

But she had a much bigger debt that had never been repaid. She shouldn't owe a single penny to that psychopath, and in turn, I shouldn't have to give him a cent of the money I worked my ass off for.

But I didn't see any other way.

I could bury this debt once and for all.

Then she might be free.

"Are you sure about this?" Carter asked as he drove through the streets of Milan at three in the morning.

Muse was asleep in the bed I shared with her. I'd snuck out in the middle of the night without her noticing. She was safe on my property, protected by gates, a security system, and a cabinet full of guns. "Yes."

"This could go badly." Carter kept one hand on the wheel while his arm rested on the windowsill. "This guy is insane. Who knows what he'll say."

"I'm not scared of him." He should be scared of me.

Carter sighed under his breath. "For the record, I'm against this."

"Duly noted."

We pulled up in front of the hotel then made our way inside. My men escorted me into the building, all carrying hand-held guns in the back of their jeans. In the basement, there was an exclusive bar that was used for business purposes only. I'd never been to the Broken Handmaiden, but I'd heard about it from Carter.

Knuckles was there, tattoos all the way up the side of his neck. He sat at a lone table in the center of the room, in a black collared shirt with a drink sitting in front of him. It looked untouched, as if he was waiting until I arrived. Each of his knuckles was marked with a different letter in black ink.

D-E-A-T-H.

The nickname suited him.

Carter and my men stayed back by the stairs as I entered the bar. Knuckles had his men against the opposite wall, their eyes trained on me. One man held an assault rifle with a finger hovering over the trigger.

Like I was meeting with any another distributor, I sat in the chair across from him then looked to the bartender. "Scotch—on the rocks."

Knuckles stared at me with bloodshot eyes, his thick arms crossed over his chest. The vein in his forehead was bigger than ever. He hated me before I even stepped into the room. If his hands weren't in plain sight, I would have worried he would pull a gun on me and shoot me between the eyes.

But he wasn't that stupid.

The silence between us was just as loud as the sound of the bartender. He grabbed a glass and then poured the amber liquid inside. He placed it in front of me seconds later.

I took a drink. "Smooth."

"Should be. It's fifty years old."

"I know wine. And you know scotch."

He finally took a drink from his glass, downing half of it before setting it down. "I hope you are here for good reason, Conway. I'm a very busy man. I have a bed full of women waiting for me upstairs. Chained to the wall with blindfolds over their eyes, they aren't going anywhere. But a gentleman should never make a woman wait."

He was as much of a gentleman as I was. "Then I'll make it quick." I snapped my fingers.

One of my men brought the black suitcase and set it on the table before he walked away.

Knuckles didn't look at it. "Care to explain?"

"It contains a million euros in cash."

He cocked an eyebrow.

"That's how much Sapphire owes you. I'm paying her debt."

His eyes narrowed farther, with displeasure rather than interest. "Yes, that's how much *she* owes me. Not you."

"Now that she's mine, her debts are my debts." The second I said the word *mine*, I became more possessive of her than ever before. I knew Knuckles wanted her chained to the wall, gagged, and covered with bruises. But she was my plaything because my pockets were a little deeper. "And I'm the kind of man who pays my debts."

The vein in his forehead appeared thicker, and the tint of his face showed his rage. "You think I'm the kind of man who will break the Underground code. So, you want to pay me off to keep me off your back?"

I noticed the way his tone deepened, the way his anger intensified. His accusation wasn't wrong, so I didn't correct it. There was nothing more insulting than when someone judged your character. But this man didn't play by the rules—not like everyone else. He was emotionally driven, which made him unpredictable and intense. "I just want to take care of my woman. I'm her man, and I don't let my woman owe anything to anyone." I finished my drink and then stood.

His eyes followed me as I moved, the corded veins in his neck swollen. His tattoos were all marked with black ink. Skulls, chains, and brass knuckles emerged from his collar. His blue eyes were the only human feature about him. The rest resembled the features of a monster.

I knew he wasn't going to say anything, so I didn't wait around for a response. I turned my back to him, exposing myself to vulnerability because I knew nothing could take me down. Then I walked out, knowing I was invincible—even to his bullets.

2

SAPPHIRE

The sheets felt cold, and the rhythmic breathing I was used to hearing was gone.

I reached over to Conway's side of the bed, looking for the chiseled physique that kept me warm through the night. I searched for that strong heartbeat, that hard body that could protect me from any storm.

But he was gone.

I opened my eyes and saw the empty spot beside me. I sat up and looked around, squinting in the darkness while I was still half asleep. I ran my fingers through my hair and did the only thing that made sense at the time. "Conway?"

No answer.

I got out of bed and checked the bathroom. Then I went into the living room, expecting to see him sitting on the couch drinking scotch. But he wasn't there either. His wallet and keys were gone, so I assumed he'd driven somewhere.

Except it was four in the morning.

Where would he go at four in the morning?

The door opened, and Conway stepped inside, dressed in a black suit with a matching tie. He looked crisp enough for a black-tie event. My eyes immediately looked at his hair, seeing it was perfectly styled like always, so a woman hadn't run her fingers through his strands. My eyes went to his collar next, looking for lipstick marks.

I hated feeling like this.

He stilled when he noticed me standing there. His pupils dilated slightly in surprise before he continued his movements. He set his phone, wallet, and keys on the table, then stripped off his jacket. "Muse, why are you awake?"

"Why are *you* awake?" I countered. "And where were you?" I flipped on the light and immediately looked at his neck, wondering if I would see bright red lipstick where a woman had kissed him. He told me we were committed now, but I couldn't think of any other reason why he was out in the middle of the night.

His eyes narrowed threateningly as he watched me stare at his neck. His anger filled the room noticeably, growing heavy in the air and entering my lungs. He didn't need to say a single word to express his ferocity. "Don't fucking look at me like that."

"I can look at you however I want," I snapped. "Who sneaks off in the middle of the night like that?"

"My business is none of your concern."

"It is when you're lying to me."

He stepped around me and tossed his jacket onto the chair. "I may be an asshole, but I'm not a liar." He turned back around and gave me a cold look. "I didn't sneak off to fuck some woman. Give me more credit than that."

"You lie to your whole family all the time. You look them in the eye and pretend this is real." My jealousy took the reins and steered me into an emotional meltdown. The idea of him being with another woman always bothered me, but now it killed me.

Now his look was completely different than it'd ever been before. He'd never looked so angry, so terrifying. "Don't. Fucking. Go. There."

"Then don't lie to me. Don't tell me it's just you and me if it's not."

"It is just you and me," he snapped. "Just because I had to leave in the middle of the night doesn't mean I was sneaking around. Now get the fuck out of my room."

"*Our* room." I crossed my arms over my chest and planted my feet. "What were you doing?"

He walked into the bedroom and ignored me. "I said, get out." He slammed the door behind him, making the walls rattle with the force.

I stayed rooted to the spot where I stood, breathing through the pain in my chest. I'd been half asleep through most of that conversation, but now I was wide awake. Maybe it was wrong of me to accuse him of sneaking around, but I'd seen those lipstick marks on his neck too many times. If he'd given me a better explanation of what he was doing, perhaps I wouldn't have jumped to conclusions.

But regardless, I was pissed.

I HAD BREAKFAST ALONE, THEN WORKED IN THE stables. But no amount of hard work could make me sweat out my anger. I was angry with Conway, and I was even angrier that he hadn't apologized.

He'd kicked me out of my own room.

After working all day, I headed back to my old bedroom and showered. It was seven in the evening, and I was starving because I'd skipped lunch. After being on my feet all day, my stomach growled, and my limbs felt weak. But I refused to eat with Conway, so I asked Dante to bring dinner to me.

When he set up two place settings at my table, I knew I wouldn't be dining alone.

Shit.

Conway walked in a moment later, dressed in jeans and a t-shirt. It didn't matter how handsome he looked, how nice his chiseled face appeared after he shaved. I was still pissed at him, still suspicious of him. Maybe I jumped to conclusions, but he gave me a reason to. He stared at me coldly as he sat across from me and dropped his napkin onto his lap.

Dante removed the stainless-steel lids from our plates, then left us alone to dine in my old bedroom.

Conway picked up his utensils and cut into his chicken, lowering his gaze to follow his movements. He didn't pretend everything was normal, but he didn't address the issue that was silently throbbing between us.

I didn't bother asking him to leave. This was his house, and despite my anger, he had all the power. All I could do was walk out myself, but I was way too hungry for that. My conversation with Andrew Lexington came back to me. He offered me a way out, a way to pay back Conway along with my other debts. I could start over and be a free woman once more. I rejected the idea instantly because I couldn't picture walking away from Conway.

But now, I was having second thoughts.

"How's your dinner?" he asked before he took a bite.

I stared at him incredulously. "We're just going to pretend last night didn't happen?"

"No." He drank his scotch. "But I assumed we would

move past it."

"So basically...pretend it didn't happen?" I snapped.

He dropped his utensils onto his plate and stared me down coldly. "What do you want to talk about? No, I wasn't out with another woman. This is a perfect opportunity for you to apologize to me for the accusation."

"Apologize?" The word could barely escape my throat because it felt so wrong. "You kicked me out of my own room."

"And I would do it again in a heartbeat. No one speaks to me that way."

"Except the woman you're living with. Yes, I will speak to you however I want. I will say the things you need to hear because I'm not a servant or an employee. I'm your woman—and I've earned the right."

Slowly, his angry expression simmered down. His eyes weren't so icy, his demeanor wasn't so cold.

"Tell me why you left in the middle of the night."

"Work."

"What kind of work would be so important?"

He drank his scotch again, his throat shifting as he swallowed. "Muse, you need to trust me."

"Why should I? You've lied to me before."

He leaned forward over the table. "You know why I lied. It wasn't because I was trying to be deceitful."

"Actually, that was exactly what you were doing."

His eyes narrowed again. "You don't need to worry about what I was doing last night. If I wanted to get laid, I would just roll you over and take you in the middle of the night. Why the fuck would I want someone else when I have you? Why would I invite you into my bedroom if I didn't want you every single night? Stop overreacting and think logically for a second. You're smarter than that, Muse. I know you are."

Maybe he was right. Maybe I was overreacting. "That doesn't explain why you won't tell me what you were doing."

"I will—just not right now."

"Why not?" I demanded.

"Because I'm not ready to."

I wanted to press him, but I knew it wouldn't get me anywhere. I was still upset about the whole thing, but I believed him. I believed he hadn't been sneaking around. I believed he was a good man and wouldn't do that to me. He had no reason to lie about his faithfulness because he could still fuck me regardless. There was no reason for him to be dishonest. "Don't expect me to apologize for what I said last night."

He picked up his utensils once more. "Don't expect an apology from me either."

We returned to eating our dinner, the tension as heavy as it was before. All we did was make eye contact while we enjoyed our meal. There was no conversation we could possibly have to fill the silence.

So, I stared at him.

And he stared back.

I GOT READY FOR BED, THEN PULLED BACK THE SHEETS on my old bed. I hadn't been sleeping with Conway long, but I was already used to it. He guarded me from my nightmares, kept me warm in the middle of the night, and protected me from the monsters lurking around the property.

Now I didn't want to sleep alone.

Even though I was still angry with him, I preferred to sleep beside him than across the hallway.

My bedroom door opened, and Conway appeared in just his sweatpants. They hung low on his hips, revealing the deep V that extended from his waist. His flat stomach was chiseled with riverbeds and mounds. He was a strong man, a powerhouse of lean muscle and tanned skin. "Muse, get your ass in here." He kept his hand on the doorknob, his presence filling the room. Then he dropped it and turned away. "Don't make me ask you twice." He left the bedroom and headed down the hall.

I could fight him just for the sake of it, but I didn't

want to. I was tired, and honestly, horny. Now, I was used to getting sex from him every single night. It was a routine we had, sex and then sleep. How would I be able to sleep without his come between my legs?

I left my bedroom and walked into his. He was already in bed with the sheets pulled up to his waist. He was scrolling through his phone, looking at emails right before bed. His eyes didn't shift my way when I walked inside. He didn't even watch me undress.

I got under the covers beside him, naked because I knew what was coming next.

He set his phone on the nightstand, then lay there, one arm behind his head with his eyes closed.

And he just kept lying there.

He didn't crawl on top of me for sex. He didn't try to kiss me. And he didn't command me to get on top of him.

He did nothing.

Maybe he was still upset with me or assumed I was upset with him. I closed my eyes and stuck to my side of the bed, waiting for sleep to overtake me. But I continued to lie there without drifting off.

I couldn't stop thinking about his sweaty chest rubbing against mine, his big cock inside me and covered with my arousal. Images flashed across my mind, and it was all I could handle. It made my body temperature rise, made my nipples harden against the sheet.

I knew he was still awake because his breathing hadn't changed. Maybe he was waiting it out, seeing if I would crack before he would.

I didn't care about winning or losing.

I just cared about getting laid.

I pulled the sheets back and moved on top of him, my legs straddling his hips and my pussy pressing against his hard cock.

His hands immediately went to my waist, and he grinned against my mouth when I kissed him. "I knew you wanted me as much as I wanted you."

"Stop talking." I didn't want his words. I wanted his kiss, that passionate embrace that made me shake all over. My spine tightened in response, and I felt my pussy clench even though he wasn't inside me yet.

He rolled me onto my back, then positioned himself between my legs. "Tell me you want me."

My hands ran up his back and into his hair. "You know I do."

His arms pinned my knees back, and he pressed his thick crown inside me. He held his face above mine, his lips almost close enough to touch. "Tell me you want me all to yourself."

I grabbed his hips and yanked him inside me, pulling that long and thick cock deep between my legs. "You're mine, Conway. I don't want to share."

He growled against my mouth before he started to thrust. "Muse..."

"I can't sleep without your come inside me."

"Fuck." He locked his gaze on to mine, his arousal so hot it burned me. "You're gonna get a lot of it tonight."

I DIDN'T WAKE UP EARLY THE NEXT MORNING TO GET TO work because I went to bed so late. Conway and I had the longest session we'd ever had, our first night of make-up sex. Neither one of us apologized to the other, but we found our way back to each other.

I still wondered what he'd been doing, but he said he would tell me, so I just had to be patient.

I woke and looked out the window to see the bright sun covering the earth. The grass looked so vibrantly green, and the horses in the pasture looked beautiful under the sunlight. My eyes moved to the terrace, where I spotted Conway sitting with his breakfast. The newspaper was open in his lap as he rested his elbows on the armrests of the cast-iron chair. His coffee sat on the saucer, and his egg white omelet was half eaten.

My first urge was to go to him, but then I decided to stay where I was. The view was perfect. The sun hit his chiseled features perfectly. His tanned skin was beautiful, and it complemented his dark hair and even darker expression. His eyes were the gateway to his kind soul, to the man underneath the monster.

I could stare at him all day.

I didn't know how things had changed so much. I came here as a woman with no freedom, but now I didn't even want that freedom anymore. When I didn't get sex, I demanded it. This man claimed my innocence, but now I wanted him to have the rest of me. I needed to listen to his deep breathing beside me in order to sleep, and anytime he was gone, I counted down the minutes until he returned.

When did everything change?

My phone rang on the bedside table.

My mind immediately went to Andrew Lexington. It'd only been a few days since our last conversation, so it couldn't be him, but so far, he was the only person in the world to ever call me on that phone. I stared at the number on the screen and recognized it.

It was him.

I took a breath before I answered the call. I continued to stand at the window in Conway's t-shirt, my bottoms still on the bedroom floor. My eyes moved to Conway on the patio. He lifted his mug without taking his eyes off his paper and took a drink. "Hello, Mr. Lexington."

"Hello, Sapphire. Please call me Andrew."

"Alright. Hi, Andrew. I thought I wouldn't hear from you for a few more days."

"Ironic," he said. "I thought I would hear from you sooner. Just wanted to pick your brain and see what you're thinking."

I watched Conway from my bird's-eye view, seeing the corded veins of his forearms. His hair was still wet and messy, obviously because he must have hopped out of the pool just a few minutes ago. I'd never seen a more beautiful man in my life. Even when he did nothing at all, he was gorgeous. A part of me wanted to walk down there and straddle his hips right under the sun.

I knew I wasn't thinking logically. I was thinking with my lust, my attraction to this man. Andrew was offering me a way out, a way to fix all my problems. I'd have to be a model again, back to never eating and being nearly naked for strangers. But at least I'd make an honest living. And at least I would have the freedom to do what I wanted. Not to mention, I would be a very wealthy woman.

But I loved being here.

I loved Conway's home. I loved his horses. I loved sharing my bed with him every night. Even if our relationship wasn't real, it felt like it meant something.

Not to mention, I'd never felt safer in my entire life.

But it wasn't real. He didn't love me. I would never be his girlfriend. He would use me until he got bored with me.

Once the inspiration ran out, he would dump me on the side of the road and find the next woman who pleased him. It didn't matter how much he aged. The older a man got, the more desirable he was. For me, time wasn't on my side.

It would be stupid not to take the deal.

Absolutely idiotic.

But I still didn't want to. "I don't think so, Andrew. I'm very flattered by your offer—"

"Two hundred and fifty million."

My mouth remained open as I heard the offer echo in my mind. He'd just added another fifty million to the pot. How could I possibly be worth that much? "Andrew, I'm a very confident woman, but I can't fathom why you think I'm worth that much."

"Trust me, you are."

"I don't know about that," I said with a chuckle.

"Take the deal, sweetheart. Any other woman on the planet would take it."

Yes, I know. And they'd be smart to. "It's not about the money."

"Three hundred."

Jesus Christ. That would leave me with two hundred million dollars for myself.

"Think about it. Please. I'm willing to do anything to make this deal happen."

"Uh..." Now I couldn't say no. But I couldn't say yes

either.

"I'll call back in a few days. Just think about how much your life would change. You would be the wealthiest model on the planet. Not only would you have fame and glory but also respect. Think about it, Sapphire." He hung up, leaving nothing but silence on the other end of the line.

I crossed my arms over my chest with the phone clutched in my fingertips. My eyes returned to Conway, who was staring across his property with a dreamy look in his eyes. He had no idea what was going on upstairs.

Now I was even more confused than before.

I SHOWERED AFTER WORKING IN THE STABLES ALL DAY. It was particularly humid that day, so sweat was smeared between my breasts and along the back of my neck. No amount of ice water could keep me cool, so when I'd finally walked into the air-conditioned house, relief had washed over me.

I stepped out of the shower and dried my hair, expecting to have dinner in our bedroom or in the dining room. I'd been thinking about my conversation with Andrew all day, trying to wrap my mind around that kind of money.

It was so much.

More than I could even fathom.

Even if I had that kind of money, what would I do with it? Conway was my only friend in the entire world, so he was the person I would turn to for advice. As a courtesy, I should talk to him about what Andrew offered me before I took it. He had the right to know what was going on. And he might know something that I didn't. Maybe Andrew was a bad man who wouldn't treat me right.

Conway was the only man I trusted.

Conway appeared in the reflection of the bathroom mirror, his shirt and jeans gone. He stood in just his boxers, muscular and ripped. His eyes were on me, green and intense, burning a hole into me. He slowly approached me until his chest was against my back. Gripping my shoulders, he then pressed a small kiss to my neck, the kind of kiss he used to give me back when we hardly knew each other. "Have dinner with me tonight."

"I have dinner with you every night."

"But this time, we're going out. Your dress is on the bed."

I held his gaze in the mirror, my reflection showing my surprise. "We're going out to eat?"

He nodded.

"Out of the house?" I asked incredulously.

He nodded again.

"We never leave the house." The only time we did was

when he had to work in Milan, and most of the time, he didn't bring me along. One of the rare times we'd left was when we visited his parents in southern Italy.

A handsome grin stretched across his face. "I'm taking you somewhere nice here in Verona."

"Wow..." I would finally get to see the city up close. I would finally see the Italian architecture and the historical footprint of this ancient city. Only in my wildest dreams had I thought I would ever be able to go sightseeing across Italy. But now, I actually could. When I wandered through the towns with just my backpack across my shoulders... Well, that was different. I slept under the stars and begged for food. It wasn't exactly fun. "I'm excited."

He kissed my shoulder again. "Be ready in thirty minutes."

THE CITY OF VERONA WAS JUST A TEN-MINUTE DRIVE from home. At sunset, it was beautiful. The unique rooftops and the winding river that moved through it made it prettier than a picture. The cobblestone streets and the architecture made it far more beautiful than any photograph could ever capture.

Conway found a parking spot, and then we walked across the street to the restaurant. He moved his arm around my waist as he guided me forward, wearing jeans and a collared shirt with the top button opened. Sunglasses were still on his nose, but once we approached the restaurant, he tucked them into his shirt.

Conway spoke to the host in Italian. It was one of the rare times I'd heard him speak his native tongue. When he was around me, he always used English. He used English at work too, probably because a lot of the models were from America.

We were guided to a table on the patio. A white candle was lit on the table, and it was close enough to the street that we could see other people walk by. But I noticed there were no other guests in the sectioned-off area. We were the only people there.

Conway pulled out my chair for me just as he did in front of his parents. Then he sat across from me and set his sunglasses on the table. His broad shoulders stretched his collared shirt, and the veins in his neck were beautiful and noticeable. Everything about him was perfect, from pretty eyes to his rugged jawline. He examined the wine menu, then set it aside, making his selection within ten seconds. Afterward, he turned to his menu.

I finally tore my gaze away from his good looks and stared at the menu, which was completely in Italian.

"Would you like me to pick something out for you?"

"Please. I trust your tastes."

The corner of his mouth rose in a smile, but he didn't lift his gaze from his menu. He looked at it for a moment longer before he set it down.

As if the waiter had been waiting for this very moment, he immediately appeared at Conway's side.

Conway ordered a bottle of wine for the table and ordered our entrees, speaking Italian for the entire conversation.

It was sexy to listen to.

The waiter disappeared with the menus, and we were alone together, sitting under the white lights of the patio while the other customers were inside.

"I'm surprised no one else wants to sit out here."

"I booked the patio." He grabbed his glass of wine that had been delivered and took a drink.

"You booked it all for yourself?"

"And you."

"You didn't have to do that, Conway."

"I did," he said quietly. "I don't like people."

His words immediately made me smile. "So, you don't like me?"

"You aren't people."

"Because I'm your property?" I teased.

"No." He rested his forearms on the table with his hands held together. "Because you're my muse. You exist on a pedestal. Everyone else is beneath you."

My smile faded away as my heart absorbed those words. It was sweet because he was honest. He had said some of the cruelest things to me, but that meant he was being honest when he said everything else—even a compliment.

I knew I should tell him about Andrew Lexington, but I'd officially chickened out. Tonight was going so well, and the last thing I wanted to do was ruin it by mentioning that his main competitor wanted to take away his biggest inspiration. It was best to wait for a better time.

The basket of bread in between us was untouched, and the nighttime breeze was filled with a nice warmth. It moved through my hair and glided down my bare back. The dress I wore was backless, black, and beautiful. He'd given me a diamond bracelet to wear, along with a necklace to match. What I was wearing was worth more money than I'd ever had in my bank account.

His fingers rested on the stem of the wineglass as he stared at me from across the table. He sat there in silence, having a conversation with me that wasn't audible. There was a constant intensity that surrounded him. Whether he was in a good mood or a bad mood, it didn't change. That was how he was—and I knew he'd inherited that from his father.

"So, how was your day?"

He didn't answer, and judging by his expression, he

wasn't going to. "There's something I want to say to you. I'm not sure how to say it, so it may come out wrong."

"Alright..." Now I knew this dinner wasn't just a random decision. It had a purpose.

"I had a conversation with my father, and I had to look him in the eye and lie to him. It made me feel like shit, made me feel worse than I ever have. And then my mother told me how proud she was of me and the man I've become."

I had no idea where this was going, but I held my breath as I listened. My fingers gripped the stem of my glass, but I hadn't taken a single drink yet. Now my appetite was curbed, and despite the dryness of my throat, I didn't want to take a drink. I just wanted to sit there and absorb every single word.

"If they knew what I did to you, they would never look at me the same. I never want to be a disappointment to my parents. Their opinion means too much to me, means the world to me. I can't go back and change what's already happened. All I can do is move forward and try to make it better."

I saw the deep connection between his family every single time I was around them. They loved each other fiercely and weren't afraid to wear their hearts on their sleeves. As rigid and stern as Mr. Barsetti was, he always showed affection toward his children.

"So, I spoke with the American authorities and paid your debts."

I stiffened at his words and almost knocked over the glass I was holding. "What...?"

"I paid back the loan you defaulted on. The bank still owns the property, but at least your credit is clear now. I also paid the property taxes you neglected. I saw that you had some student loans, so I took care of those as well."

Speechless, I stared at him with the strongest feeling of shock I'd ever known. "Conway... My loans aren't your problem. You didn't need to do that—"

"Let me finish."

I shut my mouth, but I had so much more to say.

"I also took care of Knuckles."

My eyes expanded. "What does that mean?" Did Conway kill the psychopath that murdered my brother?

"I paid back the money your brother owed him. That's where I was the other night, meeting him in Milan. I put the cash in a briefcase and left it on the table. Now he has no reason to ever bother you again. Your debt is repaid. You're free."

This was an even bigger shock than the first thing he said. "Conway..." I felt moisture build up in my eyes instantaneously. I've been running for so long that I didn't know how it felt to be safe. I'd needed Conway for protection, but now I could do whatever I wanted. I could even return to New York if that was what I wanted.

Conway's expression didn't change, even though I was falling apart right in front of his eyes. "Now that I've destroyed your demons, there's nothing chasing you. You don't owe anyone anything—and you're a free woman. And to make up for the horrible things I did to you, I'm also letting you go."

"What?" He'd paid a fortune to save me from Knuckles, and now he was just going to let me walk away? I'd only been living with him for a few months. That wasn't enough time for him to get his money back. "You want me to leave? I thought you needed me for inspiration? I don't understand..."

"No, I don't want you to leave." He kept his voice low even though there was no one nearby to hear us. It was just the two of us under the stars in the most romantic city in the world. "I want you to stay with me. But I need it to be different. I need you to stay because you want to stay, Muse. I don't want you to be my prisoner anymore. You don't owe me anything." His hand slid across the table until it rested on mine. "I need you to be my equal. I need to treat you better. I need to be the man you deserve."

His fingers felt warm the second he touched me. I could feel his slow pulse and the steady confidence in his veins.

"I don't want anything to change, but it has to be different. I want you to be here because you want to be here, not because you feel obligated to stay. So, if you want to leave, I won't stop you."

Conway unbound the shackles around my ankles and wrists. He dropped the debt I owed him. He removed all the obstacles in my way so that I could walk away without tripping. He gave me a gift I never expected him to give.

"But I want you to stay, Muse. More than anything." He held my gaze, his look deep and intense. "I want you to be the woman in my bed every night. I want you to be the woman who inspires all my pieces. I want you to be a part of me, just as you are right now." His fingers grasped mine, and he brushed his thumb over my knuckles. "What do you say?"

I didn't need to think twice about it. Even when a huge pile of money was thrown on the table, I still hesitated. Spending my days with Conway was the most comfortable I'd ever been. He satisfied me during the day as well as at night. He made me feel good in so many ways. I felt my heart aching for him, had felt it for a while now. "Before I answer, I have to ask a few things."

"Alright." He didn't hide his disappointment, obviously hoping I would agree right off the bat.

"You say you want me to stay...but what exactly do you mean by that?"

"I don't want anything to change. That's what I mean."

"So...am I your girlfriend?" Did that mean this was officially a romantic relationship? What were we?

"I said I didn't want anything to change, so we aren't really anything. We're just a man and a woman. We enjoy each other's company and have good sex. It's not more complicated than that. We're still exclusive. I'm the only man between your legs. You're the only woman in between mine."

"But is there a chance this will go somewhere?"

All he did was stare.

"You know... Well, will this turn into something serious?" I didn't want to ask if marriage and kids were on the table because that felt like too much. But was there a possibility that it could happen? That love could happen?

"I don't know what will happen, Muse." He suddenly pulled his hand away.

And that left me feeling cold. "I just... I love living with you and being with you. I just hope that it means there's a possibility of a future. That's all."

"I don't like to think about the future. Life will flash before your eyes in a nanosecond. I like to live in the present. And right now, I want you."

"So, what exactly do you want, Conway? You want me to live with you for a while, and then when things turn stale, you'll ask me to move on? But now I can leave whenever I wish?" I spoke with a toneless voice, but I felt the pain deep in my chest. I wasn't sure why I felt any pain at all. I already knew how this would go.

"I guess," he answered. "Like I said, I don't want anything to change. I just want you to be with me because you choose to be with me. The door is always open if you want to move on. So, if you're ever unhappy, I have no power over what you do. Our relationship can be based on honesty and intimacy, just as it was before."

Now I could leave Conway if I wanted to, but the truth was, I didn't want to. I could return home and finish my education, but that didn't sound appealing. I wanted to spend my time in his beautiful home, living out my days in luxury with this beautiful man. Now I would be treated with respect. Now I would have choices. I could stay for as long as I wanted, and if I didn't see it going anywhere, I could walk away.

But I knew I couldn't walk away now. "I want to stay."

His face didn't melt into a smile, but his eyes showed a new kind of intensity. He reached across the table again and gripped both of my hands, giving them a firm squeeze with his masculine strength. "I was hoping you would say that."

"But I have one condition."

"Alright."

"When people ask, you tell them I'm your girlfriend." I

didn't want to be introduced as his model or by my first name. If I was going to live with him and have this relationship with him, he needed to give me something in return.

He considered it in silence, his fingers still interlocked with mine. "Okay."

I PULLED ON THE BLACK LINGERIE THAT WAS SITTING on the bed when I walked inside. Conway purposely waited in the hallway, a bulge in his pants. He leaned against the wall with his arms crossed over his chest, like he was restraining himself from touching me.

I pulled on the black dress and felt the push-up bra press my tits together tightly. It stopped at my hips, showing off the black thong that hugged me perfectly. A large jewel was in the center, matching the diamonds I wore around my neck and on my wrist. I fixed my hair in the mirror before I got on the bed. I didn't know what kind of pose would look sexy, so I got on my hands and knees, showing off the deep curve in my back.

Conway walked inside a moment later, his collared shirt gone, and the top of his jeans undone. He looked at me with approval as he approached the bed. With a designer's eye, he examined the lingerie as it clung to my body perfectly. He looked at every curve, at every area where the fabric hung from me. He dropped his jeans and boxers at the same time, revealing his biggest tool.

His cock used to intimidate me. Even without having seen another cock in the flesh, I knew it was much bigger than average. If all men were that endowed, then men would never have a hard time getting laid. Not only was his thick, but it was exceptionally long. I wasn't even certain how it fit inside me.

He moved behind me and pressed kisses up my spine all the way to the back of my neck. He breathed against my skin, his desire heavy in the way he panted. His lips tugged against my skin, and when he reached my hair, he pressed a kiss to my ear. "On your back."

I rolled over and rested my head against the pillow. We were always doing it missionary, so I figured he would want me in a different way. He used to fuck me from behind or demand blow jobs. But now, every night we did it the same way—not that I was complaining.

He pressed my feet against his chest then pulled the thong over my hips. When I lifted my bottom off the bed, he pulled the fabric down my long legs and off my feet. Feeling the fabric in his hands first, he then rubbed my panties against his length.

I automatically bit my bottom lip.

His eyes remained on me as he jerked himself with my

panties. "You like that, Muse?"

"Yes."

He tossed my panties on the bed then moved between my legs. He held his body on top of mine, all the weight on his arms. His face hovered over mine as he sank into my cunt, inching through my slickness until his entire length was shoved inside me.

My ankles locked together against his back, and I writhed underneath him, feeling his full package stretch me so far. I breathed against his mouth, quivering because it hurt so good. I loved the way it hurt now. I loved the way the stretching was always a little too much. It made me admire his dick even more, that he was so big he could barely fit inside me. It didn't matter how many times he fucked me, I could never stretch out for him—not that I wanted to.

He started to rock into me, holding back his kiss so he could look at me instead. He watched me enjoy him, watched me breathe through the pain so I could focus on the pleasure. His hips moved gently, seating his dick deep inside me every time. It was slow and sensual, exactly the way I liked him to make love to me. "Conway..."

He pressed his forehead to mine as he moved with me, his eyes trained on mine. His arms flexed as he held his weight on top of me, and I could feel his ass tighten against my heels with every thrust. "Muse."

I pressed my mouth to his and sucked his bottom lip, already feeling my body tighten around him. My cream covered him completely, building up at the base of his cock. I was so wet for him that I could hear the sound of our sexes gliding together. My arms wrapped around his shoulders as I kissed him, my hips moving back with him as he thrust into me. "God..."

He ground into me harder, the muscles of his arms bulging from the blood flow. He gave it to me deeper, gave it to me harder. "Come for me. So I can come for you."

I gripped his shoulders and rocked back into him, my cunt taking his cock as much as possible. The harder we moved together, the more he stretched me. My slickness drenched his cock, making it easier for him to move in and out. The climax hit me hard and without notice. I exploded powerfully, my head rolling back and my body taking over. I spiraled into a craze of pleasure, a wave of goodness that made me see heaven and beyond.

No other man could ever make me feel this good.

Conway gave his final pumps as I finished. He shoved himself completely inside me and released, stuffing me full of his seed. A concentrated expression washed over his face as he finished, sexy and possessive. He claimed me without saying a single word. He told me I was his with just that single look.

I felt the come fill me, felt the warmth and the

heaviness. I was used to his cock stretching me, and now I lived for this goodness between my legs.

He kissed me as his cock softened inside my pussy, his embraces soft and gentle like the lovemaking we'd just shared. "I'm gonna give you more, Muse. Just give me a few minutes."

WHEN I WOKE UP THE NEXT MORNING, CONWAY was gone.

The clock on the nightstand said it was nine, so I knew he had already had his morning swim as well as breakfast. He was either in his office or the studio by now.

I walked into the sitting room and found my breakfast waiting there. The stainless-steel lid covered my food, and the silver pot kept my coffee warm. I poured some into my mug and then turned on the TV.

My phone was sitting on the coffee table, so I stared at it for a few minutes before I made a call.

It rang three times before Andrew answered. "Sapphire, I'm so glad to see that you've reached out to me. I'm happy to have you on board, and I think you're going to love it here in New York. From what I understand, it's your hometown, right?"

I dodged his question altogether because I didn't want

to waste his time. "Andrew, I really appreciate the offer you've given me. Truly, I'm flattered. As a woman who's never had more than a few hundred bucks in my checking account, I can't even understand that kind of money. But I'm going to have to turn you down. Before you make another offer, I want you to understand it's not about money. Conway is the man I'm sleeping with, and it would be a betrayal of our relationship if I were to work with you. And he's a man I would never betray." I was walking away from a lifetime of security to be with this man. I didn't even understand why. I wasn't in love with him. Maybe I was just connected to him because he was the first man I'd ever been with. "I'm sorry, Andrew."

Instead of trying to persuade me again, he let it be. "I understand, Sapphire. When things are personal, it's difficult to talk business. But if you ever change your mind, even if it's a year from now, I would love to hear from you. Please give me a call."

I didn't expect him to extend that kind of luxury. If Conway got bored with me, I'd still have an opportunity with Andrew. But the thought of Conway actually leaving me made me so sad that I didn't even care about that possibility. "Thank you for understanding, Andrew. Goodbye."

3
CONWAY

Now that Muse lived with me of her own free will, it rid me of my guilty conscience.

She was with me because she wanted to be here—not because she had to be.

I removed the chains binding her to me, but instead of running off, she stayed by my side. Her debts had been paid, and her nightmare had been eradicated. So, there was no other reason to be with me unless she wanted to be there.

That made the sex even better.

I worked in the studio all day, my mind stimulated by my newfound relationship with Muse. I guess she was my girlfriend, even though I'd never had one before. I wouldn't say we were in a relationship, and I couldn't picture us ever being anything more serious than what we were.

But that shouldn't surprise her.

She was my inspiration, my muse, and my mistress. Nothing more.

The only difference was, she wasn't my prisoner anymore. She was sleeping with me because she wanted me between her legs. Muse could leave and sleep with anyone, but I was the only man she wanted.

I was the only man who deserved her.

I constructed another piece that day, a royal blue bodysuit with white stones in the fabric. It would look wonderful against her tanned skin, and if she were standing on my yacht in the Mediterranean, she would be absolutely lovely.

I'd have to take her some time.

It would have to be after the show in New York. Right now, my schedule was just too busy.

Around seven, she knocked on my door. "Can I come in?"

I stood in front of the mannequin, adding the finishing touches to the design. It was simple, the blue color doing most of the creative work. The color was so stunning that it would steal anyone's focus. The material was mixed with nylon, making it stretchy but stiff at the same time. Once it was stretched across her beautiful tits, the curves would be even more hypnotic. "Of course."

She stepped inside, wearing a long white dress with a

red rose floral pattern. Her hair was pulled up in a clip, revealing the beautiful skin along her collarbone. She wore the same diamond necklace I'd given her last night. When I had a model living with me, it was hard not to dress her up. "Wow, that's beautiful."

"Thank you."

She stepped closer to the mannequin and examined it with her hands on her hips. "I really like it. Where did you come up with this?"

"I have a yacht off Mykonos. I've considered taking you on a trip along the Greek islands, and when I think of that, I picture you wearing this, looking stunning against the white buildings and the backdrop of Santorini. And I picture fucking you in that deep blue sea."

A slight blush came over her cheeks, just the way it always did when I flattered her. Now that she was growing less innocent, it was more difficult to do. But when it did happen, it was beautiful. "That sounds like a nice trip."

"You'd love it, Muse." I set the pins on the table and stood back to admire the piece. "Put it on for me."

She didn't hesitate before peeling off the nice dress she wore. When she was just in her panties and the diamond necklace, she pulled on the bodysuit, the deep V in the front showing the cleavage of her tits. Paired with her nude sandals, it was perfect on her.

I crossed my arms and leaned against the table,

examining her under the natural light of the setting sun. It looked even better on her than I imagined. The color was perfect, and the fabric was made for those curves.

"What do you think?" She posed for me, pivoting before she turned around.

"You know what I'm thinking." My cock was hardening in my jeans, and if I weren't in a hurry to get this to Nicole, Muse would be on my table right now, her legs spread and her screams echoing down the hallway. "But I need to give this to Nicole as soon as possible." I snapped my fingers, telling her to remove it.

I got a dirty look in response.

Old habits died hard. The corner of my lips rose in a smile. "Could you please remove it?"

Softness entered her expression. "That's better."

NICOLE STOOD BESIDE ME AS WE EXAMINED THE models wearing the seven different pieces I'd created. The women stood with their shoulders back and their tummies tucked in. Their legs were slightly extended, showing the toned muscle and the flawless skin. Their heels were sky-high, so only experienced runway models could handle the discomfort.

They were all beautiful, but they didn't have the same effect on me that Muse did.

I saw gorgeous women all the time. It was a regular part of my day, so I was used to it. I didn't walk around with a hard-on in my slacks all day long. I didn't even feel aroused when I looked at Lacey Lockwood in my lingerie. I guess I had become desensitized to it.

But when it came to Muse, I was never used to it.

She got me so damn hard every single time.

I stood with my arms crossed over my chest, noting the way Lacey glared at me with open venom. She was still pissed at me after our last conversation, and she wasn't pleased that Muse took the spotlight from her.

Like I gave a damn.

Nicole finally announced her judgment. "They're perfect. Each one is unique and beautiful. Whether she's on a vacation or just spending the night in a man's bed, she has the perfect ensemble to wear."

"I agree."

"I say we debut them in New York next week. I didn't think you'd be able to top your last line, but you've proved me wrong—like always."

I liked Nicole because she was real. She said what was on her mind, but she also spoke very little. She did her job well and gave me my space. If she spoke out against me, I knew it was in my best interest. She was a great assistant to have. She was so good I really didn't consider her to be an assistant at all.

I slid my hands into my pockets and studied the models a moment longer, thinking of the exact jewelry I would have them wear. Jewelers usually asked to sponsor the show by loaning their finest pieces for my girls to wear. It gave them exposure and allowed my girls to wear million-dollar diamonds without my having to drop a single euro.

"Are you going to put Sapphire in the show?" She asked the question in front of the models, and collectively, they all wore the same glare. They were united in their hatred of Muse, their jealousy clouding their judgment.

I ignored Nicole. "Thank you, ladies."

They took the dismissal and walked into the dressing room where they could strip off their pieces. When they were out of earshot, I turned back to Nicole. "Sapphire won't be modeling for Barsetti Lingerie ever again."

"Ever?" she asked incredulously. "People expect to see her at the next show. Even weeks after the last show was over, everyone was still talking about her. I think it would be a mistake not to use her. She's your inspiration for a reason."

I turned my gaze to the floor-to-ceiling window and watched the light hit the glorious city. Ancient and beautiful, it was a capital of artistic renovation. I could stare at it for hours and get lost in the details of the historic buildings. "No."

"No?" she asked. "Why not?"

I wanted Muse to wear my lingerie for me—and only me. I'd seen the way men gawked at her when she was on the runway. The way they fantasized about her. They harbored the same obsession I did—because she was the sexiest woman on the planet.

I didn't want anyone to look at her like that but me.

I turned back to Nicole. "She's retired. That's why."

"But—"

"I won't change my mind, Nicole. I was the greatest lingerie designer before her. I'll still be the greatest after her." I left Nicole in the studio and walked down the hallway to my office. Muse was inside, probably sitting on the couch reading a magazine.

Lacey Lockwood appeared in front of me, dressed in a sundress with her hair in curls. She'd changed out of the black piece in less than two minutes, probably because she wanted to intercept me in the hallway. "Conway." She moved into me to kiss me on the cheek.

Muse admitted her jealousy to me, and anytime she saw lipstick marks on my neck, she lost her mind. I wouldn't want a man kissing her, so now I honored her request by stepping back and making sure Lacey didn't have the opportunity to touch me. "You looked beautiful in that piece. I know the audience will love it in New York." I deflected the blow by complimenting her. Lacey cared about her career more than anything, and by giving her one of my best pieces, it would give her what she wanted.

But it didn't put out the fire in her eyes. Smoke emanated from the sizzling of her irises. "What is this? You demote me in your last show, and now you won't let me touch you? Is this because of *her*?" Lacey's eyes darkened in intensity, her anger exploding.

"You'll be the finale in New York, Lacey. So, don't worry about Sapphire."

"She's not in the show?"

"No." Now that Muse was gone, there was no reason for the other models to be jealous. No need to feel threatened.

Instead of making her feel better, she seemed to feel worse. "But she's still around?"

I didn't owe Lacey an explanation, so I stepped around her and walked away.

She didn't come after me, but I knew she wouldn't take this well. Lacey had made advances on me before, but I never caved. She didn't want me for me, just what I could do for her career. But even if she wanted a single night with me, it wouldn't change anything.

I never mixed business with pleasure.

I stepped inside my office and found Muse sitting on

the couch. She was in a red dress Dante had picked up from one of my favorite designers in Milan. With short sleeves and a subtle texture, it was simple. But she didn't need anything loud, not when she was so naturally beautiful.

She looked up from her magazine, her legs crossed and a diamond necklace around her neck. "How'd it go?"

"Nicole liked everything. The show is booked."

"Great." She closed the magazine and set it aside. "It's next week?"

"Yep." I walked to my desk and grabbed my tablet off the surface. Nicole updated my calendar, so I glanced through the schedule for the following week. The show would take place in New York City, to be aired on a major television network. Other designers would be there in the hope of networking with me. There was no doubt that Andrew Lexington would be there too. I would have to keep him away from Muse.

I wasn't letting anyone take her away from me.

"Will I be staying here?"

I set the tablet down then turned to her, my eyebrows rising in surprise. "To do what?"

She shrugged. "I just wasn't sure if I was invited."

I walked to the couch, my hands resting in my pockets. I stopped in front of her and placed two fingers underneath her chin. I slowly lifted her head until her neck was craned to meet my gaze. "Where I go, you go." My thumb brushed across her bottom lip, and I gently tugged it to reveal her bottom teeth.

Her mouth slowly stretched into a smile. "Will your models like that?"

"I don't give a damn what they like."

Her smile widened. "You're sure you don't want me in the show?"

"You are in the show—but I'm the only person in the audience." I dropped my hand from her chin and pulled her to her feet. My arms circled her waist, and I rested my forehead against her, surrounded by her flowery smell. She looked beautiful in everything I picked out for her, and she looked even more beautiful in just her skin. I'd never had a woman in here besides Nicole. But then again, I'd never had a woman live in my home with me either.

Muse was changing my life in drastic ways.

"Ready to go?" I asked.

Her arms rested in the crooks of my elbows. "I like it when you ask me. It's nice."

I preferred to boss her around, but I was trying to be a better man. It wasn't easy. I was used to barking out orders and watching people carry them out instantly. That kind of power was addictive, and it was never easy to wean off it. But a part of me enjoyed watching her want me, watching her choose to be with me. She could be with any other man

Lady in Lingerie

in the world, but she chose me. "I don't. But I'll keep doing it."

She smiled. "At least you're honest. And yes, I'm ready to go."

My hand intertwined with hers, and I walked with her into the hallway. A group of models was huddled together against the wall, talking quietly. They usually worked out and shared their meals together since they had such rigorous routines. I walked by with Muse, ignoring them and the way they stared at our clasped hands.

Muse didn't look at them, her eyes on me.

When we turned the corner, Nicole emerged. "Conway, I just got off the phone with a fabric distributor in Turkey. He's in the country and was wondering if you would have dinner with him tonight."

I kept walking, pulling Muse with me. "Why?"

"He said he can give you a better deal on the fabric—and provide better quality." Her heels clapped against the hardwood floor as she walked beside us. She glanced at our hands then turned her focus back to her tablet. "Is that something that would interest you?"

I was happy with my fabric and the pricing. "How much of a deal are we talking?"

"He said he can save you twenty-five percent."

Twenty-five percent wasn't pocket change. That was a

significant difference. I stopped walking, my interest officially piqued. "What time?"

"Seven. Shall I tell him you're coming?"

If this man could really deliver, it was worth the conversation. "Name?"

"Androssi Beaucount," Nicole answered. "I looked into him. He's legitimate."

I trusted Nicole. "Alright. I'll be there."

Nicole nodded and walked away.

Muse and I walked out and headed to my Ferrari, which was parked at the curb. We got inside and headed out of Milan.

Muse's dress rose to her thighs when she sat down, revealing her sexy, tanned skin. She looked out the window with her hair flowing down her chest, oblivious to just how sexy she looked in that moment.

I kept one hand on the wheel and rested the other on her thigh. Her skin was warm to the touch and so damn soft. My fingers itched to move farther up her legs, to approach the apex of her thighs and get her wet so I could fuck her when we got home.

She glanced at my hand before she looked out the window again. "Am I coming along to this meeting?"

"No." She'd stay home until I returned. By the time I was done talking business, she would have been asleep for a few hours. But that wouldn't stop me from waking her up for some action.

"Why not?"

"It's just business. Nothing that concerns you."

She turned her vicious gaze on me, clearly unhappy with that response. "What happened to where you go, I go? You just said it ten minutes ago."

"An international trip, yes. What would I do without you? My cock isn't going to want my hand now that it's had your pussy."

"I'm interested in your work. Don't businessmen bring their mistresses everywhere they go? I thought having a pretty woman on your arm made you more powerful?"

I glanced back and forth between her and the road. "Why do you want to come so badly?"

"Maybe I just like being with you. I'm your girlfriend, aren't I?"

It was just a label she demanded. I didn't agree with the definition. "I don't like it when people stare at you."

"And the only way to prevent that is by keeping me locked up all the time? That's not how I want to live, Conway." She never expressed a threat, but a hint of it burned beneath the surface.

It was one of those times I regretted granting her freedom. "Fine."

She smiled in victory then looked out the window.

Fuck, it turned me on when she bested me. My hand

slipped between her thighs until I felt her cotton thong. My fingertips pressed against her clit, feeling that little nub I loved to kiss and grind against.

Her knees immediately came together as her breathing picked up.

"Open your legs."

She didn't obey, her bright eyes turning to me.

"Now."

She parted her knees slowly, succumbing to the authority in my voice.

My fingers rubbed her harder as I kept my eyes on the road. Maybe I had to treat her like a free human being, but that didn't apply at times like these. My fingers circled her clit, and within minutes, I felt her dampness spread through the fabric. Her breathing grew deeper, and she slowly ground against my fingers.

I loved feeling that pussy grow wet because of me.

I kept working her clit as we drove through the countryside and headed to my home outside of Verona. When we were five minutes from the house, her panties were totally soaked. She was whimpering like she wanted more, wanted me to give her enough to explode. If I kept going any longer, she would climax, and I would be subjected to the torture of listening to it.

I moved my hand back to her thigh, my fingertip wet from her arousal.

Lady in Lingerie

A quiet scream erupted from her throat. "Conway..."

"You can wait until we get home."

She looked out the window, her eyes still heavy with sex. Then she dug her fingertips down the front of her thong and touched herself.

Jesus Fucking Christ.

Her head rolled back against the leather seat as she rubbed her clit aggressively, her breathing deep and rugged.

I gripped the steering wheel so tightly my knuckles started to ache. "Muse."

With eyes closed and her mouth open, she said my name. "Conway..."

"Thinking about me?"

"Yes..."

I grabbed her wrist and tugged it away. "You can wait."

"I don't think I can. You started it, Conway. Now you better finish it...or let me finish it."

I gripped her hand and felt the arousal against her skin. My skin was still wet from her slickness, so I felt the moisture between us. "You're going to wait, Muse. If you're going to undermine me, you're going to have to pay for it in other ways..."

"How much longer?"

I glanced at the villa we just passed, recognizing the

property because I'd been driving past it for ten years. "Five minutes."

She growled under her breath.

"That's what you get."

"Do you torture all your women like this?"

All the other women in my life were one-night stands or short flings. They didn't live with me or sleep with me for months on end. There was no need for torture because I didn't have enough time to tease them. We were both anxious to fuck, so we fucked hard. "Just you."

MUSE WORE A SHORT BLACK DRESS WITH THE DIAMOND necklace around her throat. Her hair was in loose curls over her chest, and the deep line plunging down the front showed a subtle hint of her tits. It was backless, the fabric covering her ass, but just barely.

I wasn't sure if I should let her go out like that.

Not when her makeup was done so well, when her eyelashes were thick with mascara, and she wore a smoky look. Her lips were painted bright red, and her foundation made her already flawless skin look unreal.

Damn, she was fine.

Everything about her was perfect, from her hourglass frame to her slender feet. She possessed the kind of beauty that didn't exist on this earth. She was made of godly qualities, like she was a Greek goddess who somehow wound up in the mortal world. An inner light seemed to shine out of her at all times. Despite her station in life and her struggle, she still held the elegance only a powerful woman could maintain. She had more strength than she realized.

She clasped her diamond earrings to her lobes then fixed her hair in the mirror. Her five-inch heels gave her an extra boost of height, but I still towered over her. When we'd come home from work, we hardly made it to the bedroom before I was inside her. Our clothes didn't even come off. My pants hugged my ass, and her dress was pushed to her hips. We fucked like we had just met at a bar and hadn't gotten laid in weeks.

I'd been fucking her for months, but it still felt like it was the first week.

She was that perfect.

Now I considered calling off this dinner as I looked at her, more interested in getting inside her than sharing a meal with a potential distributor. Saving money didn't seem as important, not when I could be inside that perfect little cunt.

She turned to me when she was ready to go, looking at me standing near the doorway. "Are you ready?"

My eyes roamed over her body, seeing the way the thin

dress hugged her so damn well. How was I supposed to pay attention to my conversation when this huge distraction was right beside me? "Yes."

She wore a soft smile as she grabbed her clutch by the door. It held her ID, the money I gave her, and the phone I bought for her. She didn't have any friends or acquaintances here, so she primarily used her phone to keep in touch with my sister.

Because Vanessa was as obsessed with her as I was.

I lingered behind as she walked into the hallway, just so I could get a nice look at her ass.

Fuck.

Now my cock was hard in my slacks even though she had satisfied me just hours before. I followed her out to the entryway. The car was ready to go, the engine on and the seats warm. It'd been washed the second I returned from Milan, keeping the paint coat shiny and new.

I sat in the driver's seat, and we headed back to Milan. We could have just stayed at my apartment as we waited for dinner, but all her clothes were in Verona. Ever since she'd come into my life, I never stayed at that apartment. It primarily had been used for my hookups in the city or as a place to sleep when I worked late. Now my glorified bachelor pad was obsolete.

Because it didn't seem like I was a bachelor anymore.

We drove through the countryside in silence, the radio

off and the world around us dark. I pushed my car to the limit, knowing I wouldn't be pulled over by the authorities since they would recognize my car. I wasn't a crime lord, but I was certainly above the law around here.

My eyes kept drifting back to her legs, the way the fabric of her dress hugged her thighs. I had sex that morning when I woke up and sex again when I got off work. There was no reason I should be so horny right now.

But this woman made me horny.

"Anything I should know before we meet this guy?" She broke the silence with her hypnotic voice.

"Just don't talk."

"Don't talk?" she asked incredulously.

"You're there to look pretty on my arm. That's your only purpose. No need for you to speak."

"Wow..." She shook her head. "Just when you're being a good man, you switch back."

"This is my business meeting, and you have no say in the matter. I'm just being direct with you."

"Can I say hi?" she snapped.

"Don't be stupid. You're too smart for that."

She looked out her passenger window, tuning me out.

I grabbed her hand and held it on her thigh, my thumb brushing along her knuckles. I refused to apologize because I had no reason to, so I let the silence stretch between us.

She would get over it eventually. After everything I did to her, she wasn't one to hold a grudge.

We arrived in Milan thirty minutes later, and when I pulled up to the restaurant, the valet took care of my car. My arm circled my woman's waist, and I walked with her inside, seeing all the heads turn my way.

Some people recognized me, mainly the women.

But everyone recognized her.

I pulled her closer into my side, proving that she belonged to me. They could look all they wanted, but I was the only one who could touch.

The host recognized my face once I walked inside, and he ignored the next people in line standing at the podium to silently escort us to the table. My hand remained on Muse's waist, squeezing her side gently because I loved the way her petite frame felt in my grasp. She'd never made a dress look more beautiful.

We found Androssi Beaucount in the secluded booth in the corner. He had a woman on his arm as well, an exotic-looking woman with deep black hair and olive skin. She had big brown eyes, and her hair was pulled back in a slick ponytail.

But she had nothing on Muse.

Androssi rose to his feet, a middle-aged man with weathered lines in his face from too much exposure to the

Lady in Lingerie

sun. He wore a polite smile and shook my hand. "Mr. Barsetti, it's a pleasure."

"Call me Conway. My father is Mr. Barsetti."

"Of course. You can call me Androssi." He turned his gaze to Muse. "Sapphire, it's a much bigger pleasure to meet you." He took her hand and leaned in.

I pressed my hand to his shoulder and steadied him. "A handshake will suffice, Androssi." In my culture, it was common for a man to kiss a woman upon meeting her. But I didn't want anyone else pressing a kiss to my woman's cheek. They should be grateful I would even allow a handshake to happen.

"Of course." He brushed off the threat and shook her hand. "Allow me to introduce Mercedes." He pulled his woman to his side. She was at least twenty years younger than him. Dressed in black with expensive jewelry, she looked like his favorite mistress.

"Nice to meet you." Muse shook her hand.

"You too," Mercedes said with a thick Turkish accent.

We took a seat in the booth, and my hand immediately went to Muse's thigh under the table. I felt her bare skin, and my fingertips came alive the second I felt her in my grasp.

Her arm hooked through mine, and she rested her hand on the crook of my elbow.

I kept my eyes on Androssi, finding his mistress plain.

"Business is good, I hear," Androssi said. "After your last fashion show, your popularity has reached a whole new level. And if you can make even more money than you were before, why wouldn't you?" He waved the waiter over, ordered a bottle of wine, and then dismissed him.

He picked a wine created by Barsetti Vineyards—because he did his homework.

Muse ran her finger across the edge of her mouth, her lipstick sticking to her skin.

I tried not to look—because it always made me think of other things. "How do you propose I make more money?"

"By cutting your costs," he said. "I know you purchase nearly all your fabrics from Ulysses in Istanbul. I'm not going to lie to you, Conway. He provides excellent fabrics at a reasonable price. It's no surprise you've been in business with him for ten years. You must have a sense of loyalty to him at this point. But when it comes to business, nothing is personal."

"And you think you can save me twenty-five percent in costs?" I challenged. "That's a lot, Androssi. I'm always interested in maximizing my margins, but not if it would dilute the quality of my products. The Duke of Cambridge commissioned me to create the wedding night lingerie for his bride. It took me a full week to create something that he'd want to rip off her. My clients aren't regular people.

They're royalty, celebrities, and world leaders. I won't tolerate anything less than the best."

Muse moved her hand on top of mine as it rested on her thigh. Her fingers rubbed against me, and I could feel her tit against the back of my arm. She was cuddled close to my side, sticking to me like glue. Her resentment toward me had obviously disappeared.

"I respect that, Conway," Androssi said. "The fabric is exactly the same. There's no compromise on the quality."

"Then how can you provide me with such a substantial deal?"

His hands came together on the table, his fingers interlocking as Mercedes enjoyed her wine in silence. She took a piece of bread and ate a few bites, not making conversation with Muse but sticking to her silence and letting her suitor do the talking. "There's actually a condition to the price—and it depends on you."

Of course, there was a catch. "How so?"

"Ever since you debuted Sapphire in your line, your creations have exploded in popularity. The people adore your main star. Women who don't have anyone to wear lingerie for are buying it, just so they can be like her. She's the greatest marketing strategy you could ever find. And I can only imagine the new heights you'll reach with her modeling your line. Your sales will skyrocket, and as your units grow, I can cut you a better deal on the price. Ulysses can't do that, but I have the equipment to make it happen."

I stared at him coldly, annoyed that Muse had been brought into the conversation when she should have been excluded. I'd been in the lingerie business for ten years, and I'd earned a reputation based on my own merit. It wasn't because of the models or the fabric—it was because of me. I had to admit that Muse gave me a significant boost. I'd be lying if I said that was untrue. But I was the one who propelled myself to greatness. "Muse is no longer modeling my lingerie. She's retired."

Androssi couldn't hide the surprise that came over his face. "Retired?"

"Yes. But I have no doubt I'll be able to raise my units with my new release—without her." She was my most erotic fantasy, and that desire carried over into my creations. Men could still make their dreams come true, even if they didn't see my greatest model on the runway. She wasn't showing her nearly naked body to the world anymore. She was only modeling for me now.

He sat back against the leather seat, the devastation obvious in his expression. "I won't tell you how to run your business, Conway. But I think that's a mistake. She's become an international sensation, a sex symbol. If she doesn't step onto that stage for your next show, I think there will be consequences."

Lady in Lingerie

"I don't give a shit what you think, Androssi."

Tension filled the air between us, his eyes narrowing in offense as my hands formed fists. Androssi would be smart to remember that he needed me a lot more than I needed him. I was one of the biggest clients in the fabric world. Acquiring me would make him a very rich man.

Muse cleared her throat. "Once Conway debuts his new line, he'll get the orders in for his pieces. Then you guys can decide how to move forward."

I'd told her not to speak, but her mediation was necessary. I'd just been insulted by this man, and then I'd insulted him in return. Only the grace of a beautiful woman could calm our anger.

Androssi's shoulders softened once Muse made her statement. "Yes, let's reconvene."

"I will get those units to you, Androssi. But now, if you want my business, it's a thirty-percent reduction."

"That's—"

"Thirty. Percent." I grabbed my glass and downed the wine before I rose to my feet, pulling Muse with me. I tossed euros on the table because I didn't want to feel like I owed this man anything. Then I stormed off.

Muse stayed behind, facing Androssi with an apologetic look. "Thank you for meeting us tonight. We'll be in touch."

I glared at her, my hand itching to grasp her waist and

pull her out of there. If she were just my property, I wouldn't refrain from slapping her across the face or yanking her out by the hair.

But that would break the promise I made to her.

I YANKED OFF MY JACKET AND TOSSED IT ON THE BACK of the chair. My tie was pulled loose and thrown on the couch. I pulled the cigars out of my drawer and lit up before I inhaled the thick smoke into my lungs. I didn't smoke often, but when I did, it killed my sour mood.

Muse yanked the cigar out of my mouth and shoved it into the ashtray. "This is poison."

"Anything good is poison." I picked up the lighter and sparked the flame.

She snatched it out of my hand as well and slammed it on the table. "No smoking, Conway. I mean it."

"Don't talk to me like you have some kind of power over me." She had no authority over what I did. I'd smoke until I got lung cancer—that was my choice. I wouldn't change my mind just because a beautiful woman asked me to.

"I do have power over you. Let's not pretend I don't."

"You're stupid if you think you do." I was speaking out of anger, frustrated that people continued to doubt my ability to deliver quality work. I was the inventor of the art. Muse simply wore it.

She peeled off her dress until it was a pile at her feet. She left on the black thong, and she slowly ripped off the tape that kept her nipples flat. Her pink mountains finally came free, immediately pebbling when they came into contact with the cool air.

I tried not to stare.

She crawled into my lap and straddled my hips, her perfectly soft body brushing against the crispness of my slacks. She unbuttoned my collared shirt, revealing my naked chest with her small fingertips. With her hair pulled over one shoulder and a confident expression in her eyes, she was absolutely stunning on my lap.

And just like that, I began to harden.

Fuck.

"No smoking." She spoke with the anger in her eyes then rage. "I mean it, Conway. All it does is hurt you."

"And what does alcohol do?"

"Alcohol is different. Smoking kills. If I ever see you with another cigar—"

"You'll what?" I challenged. "Slap me on the wrist?"

"No." Her nails dug into me threateningly. "I'll take away the one thing you love most."

She didn't need to spell it out for me because I knew exactly what she was referring to.

Her.

"So, no smoking," she repeated. "And you need to calm down."

"I told you not to talk at dinner."

"And you thought I would listen?" she asked incredulously. "You were a complete ass. I had to smooth things over."

"Why?" I snapped. "He's just some distributor. You think I care about pissing him off?"

"A man should go out of his way to make friends, not enemies." She opened my shirt to reveal more of my chest. "Don't burn bridges, Conway. Number one lesson in business. At least, that's what I learned."

I held her gaze and refused to back down. It was easy to get lost in her eyes, to get lost in the painful beauty of her face. But no matter how beautiful she was, I refused to cave. I would never admit she was right—ever.

"You should put me in the show next week."

My eyes scanned over her face, finding the sincerity in her look.

"You said I'm free, and I'm doing this willingly. Besides, you paid for me. You should get some use out of me."

"I told you that you didn't owe me anything," I whispered. "And no, I don't want you parading around half

Lady in Lingerie

naked so men can jerk off to you later. You're mine—and I don't share. End of story, Muse."

"I thought your work was the most important thing to you?" she challenged.

"It is. And it'll do just fine without you. You've inspired my creations—and that's as close as people are going to get to you." If I couldn't handle someone kissing her on the cheek, even my own cousin, then I wouldn't be able to handle a room full of people staring at her. I wouldn't be able to handle the whole world staring at her. I'd never had her photographed because I didn't want that either—for the world to have a piece of her.

I owned all of her.

"I'm going to bed," I said, silently asking her to get off me.

She didn't move, sitting on my dick purposely. She shook her hips slightly, grinding against me. She could feel my length through my slacks because my size was unmistakable. "Doesn't seem like you want to go to bed."

"I'm hard, but I'm also angry. And I'm angrier than I am hard."

She undid my belt and unbuttoned my slacks. She flipped her hair over her shoulder, her tits shaking with her movements. "Tell me your fantasy, Conway. I want to please you. I want to give you what you want…"

I breathed through my teeth and felt my cock twitch in

betrayal. Having her as a prisoner turned me on, but listening to her ask how to make me feel good was so much better. She could be anywhere in the world right now—but she wanted to sit on my lap.

"Tell me what you want."

My hands snaked up her legs toward her hips. I gripped her tightly, feeling her slender waistline. It always surprised me how soft her skin was to the touch. Despite how callused my hands were from using them for a decade, I could still detect the differences in texture. I could still study her body at an intimate level, still feel the bumps as they sprinkled across her skin.

I could ask for something kinky since the offer was on the table. I could ram my dick in her ass and listen to her cry through the pain. I could spank her ass with my eager palm and leave a handprint right on her skin.

But instead, I wanted to be just like this, with her beautiful eyes transfixed on mine. When her gorgeous tits were in my face like this, it was hard to argue for a different position. The anger I felt just moments ago faded away as I considered her request. Rage didn't seem important when she could make me feel something so much better. "I want you... Just like this."

THANK YOU

Every item you buy or donate
helps beat poverty.

We are happy to offer a 30 day refund policy for items returned to the store in the same condition they were sold in, with proof of purchase and with a valid price ticket attached to the item.
View full T&C's in store or at: **www.oxfam.org.uk/shoptags**
This does not affect your statutory rights.

Oxfam is a registered charity in England and Wales (no 202918) and Scotland (SC039042).
Oxfam GB is a member of Oxfam International.

Find thousands of unique
items in our online shop
www.oxfam.org.uk/shop

THANK YOU

Every item you buy or donate

beat poverty for good
www.oxfam.org.uk/volunteer

OXFAM

VAT: 348 4542 38

Volunteer here: Have fun,
meet new people & learn
new skills
Sign up in-store or at
www.oxfam.org.uk/jointhe team

KAREN	SALES	F2924/POS1

TUESDAY 21 NOVEMBER 2023   16:19 245809

GIFT AID 20121475519999
2 x £1.99
2 FICTION BOOKS   £3.98

2 Items

TOTAL   **£3.98**

CREDIT CARD   £3.98

Oxfam Shop: F2924
5, The Bridge,
Chippenham, SN15 1HA
01249 447061
oxfam.org.uk/shop

4
SAPPHIRE

I was wrapped up in the warmth that Conway's body produced. It filled the sheets and acted as a personal heater. Even if the house lost power in a storm, his physique would be enough to get us through the night.

My arm was draped over his hard stomach, and my face rested against his shoulder. I could feel the steady rise and fall of his body. Even when he was asleep, his body remained rigid and hard.

His alarm went off.

I didn't open my eyes because I was way too comfortable.

Conway didn't respond right away. He lay there, letting the beeps fill the room. He finally reached over and hit the button so the noise would stop. He cleared his throat slightly then ran his fingers through his hair, slowly waking up after the peaceful night we'd both just had. We had sex in his chair then immediately went to bed, once the anger had been completely wiped away from his thoughts.

He turned his head my way. I could feel his stare even though my eyes were still closed. I'd been the recipient of that look so many times that I recognized it the second I felt it. He leaned down and kissed me on the forehead, his warm lips soft against my skin. His mouth tugged slightly on my skin before he pulled away and sat up.

I still didn't open my eyes, but I released a quiet protest. "Mmm…"

He hesitated. "You want me to stay?"

"Yes…"

"I've got a lot of work to do, Muse." His hand moved into my hair.

That was when I finally opened my eyes. I stared at the sleepiness in his eyes, seeing his ruffled hair and rested expression. His tanned skin was such a pretty color, a color only a true Italian could acquire.

He gave me a slight smile before he got out of bed, his bare ass right in my line of sight.

Such a beautiful ass.

He changed into his swimsuit and grabbed his goggles before leaving the room.

I knew I should get up so I could have breakfast before

I headed to work. And if I got up right now, I could watch him swim a bit. When those drops fell down his body, it was an arousing sight. It was even tastier than breakfast.

I sat on the terrace under the umbrella because it was already hot despite the morning sun. We were making our way into fall, but the heat hadn't died away yet. I enjoyed my coffee as Conway completed his morning fitness routine. My phone was on the table even though the only person who ever contacted me was Vanessa.

Conway climbed out and dried off with a towel, water streaking down his hard physique. No matter the angle, he was chiseled and strong. His muscular shoulders led to cut arms, and his large pectoral muscles contrasted with his narrow hips. He was a perfect triangle, the ideal example of masculinity. Never in my life had I looked at a man and felt the kind of physical attraction I did for him. The second I saw him on TV, he became my celebrity crush. But now, I was the woman sleeping in his bed every night, the only woman in his life at the moment.

Life could be unpredictable.

He finished off by drying his hair with a towel before he joined me at the table.

The second his ass was in the seat, Dante appeared

with breakfast platters. There was a baguette of fresh French bread, a side of fruit, and an egg white crepe with vegetables and marinara sauce. It was more carbs than he usually ate, so today must be a cheat day.

He'd definitely earned a cheat day.

He grabbed the newspaper and started reading.

I sipped my coffee and stared at him, enjoying the view of him sitting across from me.

When he felt my stare, he glanced up. "Yes?"

"Yes, what?"

"You're staring."

"So?"

His eyes flicked down again. "It's rude."

"It's not rude when you do it?"

"It's different."

"No, it's exactly the same. And I like to stare at you." I held my coffee between my hands and took a sip. "You're hot."

His eyes moved up again, this time accompanied by a smile. "Hot?"

"Yeah."

His grin quickly turned into an arrogant one. "I guess I should have put out this morning."

"You should always put out."

His smile dropped instantly, his eyes suddenly

Lady in Lingerie

darkening in intensity. He stared at me for several heartbeats, his newspaper still open but forgotten.

I smiled then sipped my coffee again, loving the way I got under his skin so easily.

After another minute passed, he finally returned his gaze to his paper. "You aren't working in the stables today."

"I'm not?"

"No. You're working with me in the studio."

"I thought you had all your pieces ready?" I quipped.

"Well, I think I just got inspiration for another one."

I set my coffee down as a small heat wave moved over my body. It had nothing to do with the coffee, but now it was too hot to hold. I ripped off a piece of bread and popped it into my mouth.

We fell into comfortable silence.

My phone rang.

I didn't recognize the number on the screen. It wasn't Andrew Lexington or Vanessa.

Conway didn't look up from his newspaper.

I took the call. "Hi, this is Sapphire."

"Hey, Sapphire." Her deep voice came over the line, affectionate and warm. "It's Pearl, Conway's mother."

My eyebrows shot up because I never expected her to call me. "Hello, Mrs. Barsetti. What a nice surprise."

Conway lowered his newspaper as his eyes settled on me.

"Oh, call me Pearl," she said with a laugh. "Mrs. Barsetti makes me feel old. I only let people call me that in public because my husband demands that's how people address me...because he's a psychopath."

I laughed at the open way she spoke about her husband, in a teasing tone with an underlying seriousness. "Reminds me of Conway."

She laughed at the joke I made about her son. "I didn't realize how similar they were until he brought you around. Anyway, I'm in the area and wanted to know if you wanted to get lunch and do some shopping."

Conway's mother was asking to spend time with me. I froze on the spot because the question was totally unexpected. I couldn't say no because that was rude, and I didn't want to say no anyway. Now that I wasn't his prisoner, just his girlfriend, it didn't seem as deceitful. "Sure, I'd love to."

"Great. I'll pick you up in a few hours."

Conway extended his hand. "Give me the phone."

"Why?" I whispered.

"Just give it to me." He snatched it out of my hand and pressed it to his ear. "Mom, what's going on?"

I could hear her voice through the phone. "Just wanted to ask Sapphire if she wanted to get lunch. Is that okay?"

"Of course, it's fine. I just didn't realize you were in town."

"Your father is meeting with a client in Verona. A bit of a last-minute thing. He's going to be busy talking about wine and money, so I thought I would find something more fun to do."

"How about I pick you up?" he asked. "We can meet you in Verona."

"Son," she said with a chuckle. "You know I love you, but I was hoping to spend the day with Sapphire. Our conversations about clothes and jewelry and our shopping spree will bore you anyway."

Conway didn't protest, but his face darkened in annoyance. "Will Vanessa be joining you?"

"No," she answered. "She has to finish a piece she's working on."

"Well, I'll drop Sapphire off to you," he said.

"I can pick her up," his mother countered. "I know you're busy, so just resume your day. Now give me back to Sapphire."

He expressed his annoyance again before handing back the phone.

"It's me again," I said once the phone was pressed to my ear.

"He doesn't like to be left out, does he?" she asked with a chuckle. "He's so much like his father that I worry he didn't inherit any of my traits."

"He's got your smile." I'd noticed that the second I met her.

"True," she said. "But too bad he's an overbearing, overprotective, and over-controlling weirdo."

I tried to cover up my laugh since Conway could hear everything we were saying.

"I'll see you in a little bit," Pearl said. "And lunch is on me."

We hung up, and I set the phone on the table.

Conway looked livid.

"What?" I asked. "I didn't call her."

With a hard jaw, he picked up his paper again.

"You're that annoyed I'll be spending time with your mother?"

"No." This time, he folded up the paper and set it down. "I just don't feel comfortable letting the two of you run around by yourselves."

When it came to me doing anything alone, he could never stand it. When Vanessa went on a date, he had her followed like something terrible could happen at any moment. Now he felt the same way about his mother. "Conway, it'll be fine."

"You should never assume. I'm disappointed my father is letting this happen."

"Letting it happen?" I asked incredulously. "Your mother doesn't strike me as a woman who lets her husband boss her around. I wouldn't like her very much if she did. You need to let this go, Conway. And if I find out you're having us followed, I'll make you regret it."

Whenever I stood up to him, he usually respected me for it. But now, he was simply livid. He didn't say another word, but his dark eyes focused on me with sinister intensity. His gaze spoke of restrained violence and all the things he wanted to say. His hands formed fists, and his jaw was so tight it seemed like it might snap.

He rose to his feet and pushed the chair away with the back of his knees. With his breakfast untouched and his mood sour like a rotten apple, he stormed off, leaving me sitting there alone.

I didn't go after him because I was far too proud. But the second he was gone, I felt the coldness that lingered behind. The warmth of the summer sun and the humid air couldn't chase away the frigidness.

Now it felt like winter.

I GOT INTO THE PASSENGER SEAT OF THE BLACK Lamborghini, and Pearl drove onto the country road.

Conway didn't say goodbye to me. He didn't even come outside to say hello to his mother. He went into his studio and didn't reemerge.

That told me he really was pissed.

Pearl drove the expensive sports car like she'd been doing it for years. She pushed past the speed limit and drove us toward the historic city of Verona. The beige buildings extended slightly above the ground, and the center of the city glowed under the sun. "It's a beautiful day."

"It's always a beautiful day here." It hadn't rained once since I'd arrived, but now that summer was over, I knew the fall would bring the chill. In winter, it would snow. It would make my job at the stables a lot more difficult.

She smiled as she drove with one hand. "You love it here, huh?"

It wasn't anything like home, but that wasn't a bad thing. "I do. I thought I wouldn't be able to live anywhere besides the city, but now I prefer the quiet countryside."

She approached Verona then slowed down as we entered the narrow streets. "I'm from New York too. Born and raised."

"Really?" I'd noticed her American accent the second we met. I assumed she was from America, but I didn't know where.

"Yeah. I went to college there and started working as an engineer for the city. I helped with the architectural design and to make sure the buildings were safe. New York has been hit with a lot of blizzards, so my job was to make sure none of them fell." She pulled into a parking spot along the sidewalk. We got out and started walking down the cobblestone street. We made a few turns, entering a walkway where cars weren't allowed.

"That's really cool," I said. "Did you like it?"

"I did," she replied. "I was passionate about my job and loved going to work every day, but once I came here, I immediately adapted to this way of life. Making wine and enjoying the sunshine is far more pleasant. So, lunch first?"

"Yeah, sure."

We walked to a small café and sat down. Our menus were brought, and we both ordered salads along with a bottle of wine. The basket in the center of the table was full of fresh bread, so we both took a few slices.

"Conway is angry, isn't he?" She swirled her wine before she took a drink.

Never underestimate a mother's understanding of her son. "A bit."

"I figured when I didn't see him walk you out." She spoke with the same positivity, like her son's attitude didn't affect her in the least. "Just ignore him. He'll come around."

"He's very overprotective. I've never met a man like that."

"Yeah, it gets annoying," she said. "My husband is the exact same way. I have to tell him off and just storm out.

But I know his concern comes from a good place, so I don't judge him for it. Conway is the same way. Stand your ground, but be understanding at the same time. He's a good man who just wants to keep you safe."

"I know. But it's a little too much sometimes. Vanessa and I went out one night, and he wouldn't let me go unless he came along. And then Vanessa went on a date and he followed her. It's excessive."

She shook her head slightly.

"I just wonder why he's so worried all the time. He's never explained his concern to me."

She looked down into her glass as she swirled the contents.

Now I knew my intuition was correct. There was a reason for his behavior, something that involved his whole family. His protectiveness had nothing to do with what happened to me. It just made it worse. "Something happened, didn't it?"

She took a drink before meeting my gaze. "It's not my place to tell. When he's ready, he'll share it with you."

My heart slowly sank into my stomach once the realization hit me. Conway had suffered in his past. Something had happened to him. His protectiveness stemmed from a legitimate event. Maybe I should have been more understanding.

"Anyway...there's a few shops I want to take you to. And has Conway showed you Juliet's balcony?"

"Sorry?" I asked.

"I'll take that as a no," she said with a chuckle. "It's rumored that this old house is where Shakespeare got his inspiration for *Romeo and Juliet*. Juliet's family were real people, and it is believed that this house was a possible setting where she really could have lived. It's now a historic landmark."

"No, I never knew that..."

"Then we'll swing by on our way. I think you'll like it."

"Yeah, that would be great."

Our salads arrived. It surprised me how easy it was for me to talk to Conway's mother since we'd never been alone together. But she was easy to get along with, completely real and transparent. I never felt judged for being a lingerie model, even though it was something a few people would think less of me for. It seemed like Pearl liked me, regardless of the fact that she didn't know me well. Since Conway had never been with another woman, maybe choosing me automatically made his decision credible. His entire family accepted me because they assumed I was the one.

"Vanessa tells me she really likes you. My daughter tends to like everyone, but she seems to like you particularly."

"She's sweet." Since Vanessa first laid eyes on me, we'd become friends. If Conway and I moved on from each other, I would probably still keep my friendship with her because I liked her so much. "She's so smart. She downplays it a lot, but I can tell she's a lot smarter than she wants people to realize."

Pearl smiled before she took a bite of her salad. "Yes, she's a very smart girl. Too smart. She's a genius like her father, but she possesses my easygoing attitude. I'm so glad she inherited that, because living with two intense men for eighteen years was too much. Just one is enough."

"What was Conway like growing up?"

"Very charismatic." She smiled as she thought back to his childhood. "He always did well in school. He was very active in sports. Very popular among the rest of the students in his class. But he was also very private. He matured much faster than the average boy his age. He seemed to come into adulthood when he was fifteen or so. By then, he was fairly independent and ready to move on with his life. The day he turned eighteen, he was ready to move out."

"He's still private now."

"He's very protective of his creative genius, not that I judge him for it. He was an easy son to raise, and I'm very proud of who he's become—even with the overbearing nature." She smiled and drank from her glass. "When he moved to Milan, it was hard for Crow. Cane has always been my husband's best friend, but Conway quickly replaced him once he was older. I know Crow was looking forward to enjoying the years of having Conway as a friend rather than a son. But since Conway lives so far away, that hasn't really happened. He pictured Conway taking over the wine business so that he could see him every day."

My eyes softened in sadness, knowing that letting a son go must be difficult. They were such a close family. Of course they wanted to be even closer.

"The hardest thing about being a parent is when your job is over. The day Conway no longer needed me, I was happy and sad. But Crow has never really gotten over it. And Vanessa is so independent that she's never wanted help from anyone. She's a very stubborn Barsetti."

Conway's studio was in Milan, but he spent most of his time in his home in Verona. But since he was the business owner, I didn't understand why he couldn't handle his company from Florence, somewhere closer to his family.

"Do you want to have children?"

The question yanked me from my thoughts. "Yes."

"How many?"

"Two," I said. "But maybe three. I'm not sure yet. Depends on when I have the first one."

"If you don't mind me asking, do you and Conway talk about that sort of thing?"

I didn't want his mother to get her hopes up, that Conway and I would get married and start a family. He said he wasn't looking for romance or anything meaningful, but I couldn't help but question our relationship. He said he didn't want monogamy, but that's exactly what we had. He said he didn't want to kiss, but now he couldn't stop kissing me. Then he gave me my freedom and asked me to stay with him. Everything he did contradicted everything he said. "It's come up a few times..."

Pearl smiled in a new way. "That's nice to hear. Conway is so committed to his career, I thought he might not want children. Crow was the same way until I became pregnant with Conway. And the second I was pregnant, he was happy."

Maybe Conway didn't realize everything he wanted. Maybe he just needed time to figure it out.

Pearl continued to eat her salad, taking small bites but not eating much. Her wedding ring was unusual because it was a white gold band with a single button on top. There were no diamonds. It was obviously one of a kind. "How did you and Crow meet?"

She hesitated in her movements, pausing before she set down her fork. "It's a long story. I'll tell you another time."

It was a weird response, but I didn't push her on it. It was her personal life, and if she didn't want to share it with me, that was her decision. "How do you like your salad?"

"It's excellent. Crow and I come here often when we're in town."

"Is he here now?"

"Yes. He's meeting with this man who owns a dozen restaurants around Verona. He's a fan of Barsetti wine, so he's interested in buying our product in bulk. We have different versions of our wines that we offer clients. Crow will go out into the vineyards and identify the largest and juiciest grapes. He'll use those in the press instead of the generic ones we harvest. As a result, the wine is a lot brighter. It's not necessarily stronger in taste, just bolder. Those wines cost more because there are only so many prime grapes in the harvest. It sounds like this man wants to exclusively reserve those cases since we only make so many every year."

"Wow, I never knew that."

"We charge a lot more for that exclusive wine, but this man is willing to pay to be the exclusive distributor of it. It's a smart move on his part and also a great deal for us. Win-win."

"That does sound great. Do you enjoy working at the winery?"

"Very much so," she responded. "I've never felt more connected to the earth than I do now. A simple life is a much better life. Our family is small, but it's certainly enough. I used to love the chaos of the city, the constant sound of people going out for Chinese at two in the morning. But now I find the silence comforting."

When I first ran to Italy, I knew it would be beautiful, but since I was on the run from a ferocious man, I never expected to really enjoy it. Now it made me wonder if I would ever want to return to New York. Conway said I was free to do whatever I wanted. But would I ever want to go back?

I wasn't so sure.

Pearl paid the tab. "Ready to shop?"

"Absolutely."

Pearl dropped me off at the front of the house and gave me a kiss on the cheek. "Thanks for spending the day with me."

"Thank you for taking me out."

"You need help with those bags?"

"No, I got it."

She kissed me on the cheek again before letting me go.

I carried my two bags out of the car along with my purse and headed to the doorway. I waved before walking inside. A part of me expected to see Conway waiting for me, but he'd obviously been locked away in his studio the entire time. We were supposed to spend the day screwing on his table, but the unexpected happened.

I thought he would be over it by now.

I returned to our bedroom and hung up the new dress I bought. I got a bracelet to go with it, and I bought a pair of heels that weren't as tall as all the others Conway bought me. At least this way I could look nice without killing my feet.

Conway must have known I was home because his footsteps sounded behind me.

I turned to face him, only to see the same pissed-off expression he wore when I left the house a few hours ago. He was in jeans and a t-shirt, the fabric hugging his chest in the sexiest way. Whenever he was angry, he somehow looked more handsome. It must have been his intensity. It used to intimidate me, but now I craved it. "I made it back in one piece, so you can calm down now."

He slowly slid his hands into his pockets, his thick arms carved out of dense stone. "Am I not calm?" He spoke the words quietly, but they were filled with cold malice. His eyes showed his aggression. Unlike other people, he didn't need to raise his voice and start screaming to get his point across. The quieter he was, the more terrifying he became.

"Not at all." I pulled the black dress out of the closet. "What do you think?"

He didn't look at it.

"I thought it fit well, and it has a nice slit right at the waistline." I turned around and hung it back in the closet. "Your mom got something nice too. You know, for a woman in her fifties, she looks pretty damn good."

"Which is why the two of you shouldn't be running around together."

I placed one hand on my hip and stood up to him just as his mother encouraged me to. "Let it go, Conway. Your mother asked me to spend time with her. I wasn't going to say no. And it wouldn't have felt the same if you were there."

He silently excused himself from the conversation and left the bedroom. He'd come in here hardly saying anything, and now he was leaving without accomplishing anything.

"Conway?"

He stopped but didn't turn around.

I crossed through the doorway and entered the sitting room. Stopping behind him, I pressed my hands to his lower back. Slowly, I moved upward, feeling the muscles of his flank through his t-shirt. I traced the grooves between his muscles with my fingertips and moved higher until I reached his shoulders.

He released a deep breath, responding to my touch.

"Tell me what happened to your family."

He took another deep breath, his back expanding slowly. "What did she tell you?"

My hands moved down again, following the lines between his muscles. I felt his strength at my fingertips, felt his power under my touch. I followed the curve of his back until I reached his narrow hips. "She told me to be understanding of your protectiveness, to be patient with you because of what your family has been through. But she also told me to stand my ground against you, to live my life to the fullest...despite your attempts to protect me from everything. She didn't say anything else or give specifics." She allowed her son the opportunity to tell me his secret. She wouldn't take that away from him.

He breathed again, this time in relief.

"Tell me, Conway. My whole family is gone, and I have nothing left. I know how it feels to suffer, to lose someone you love. I know how it feels to be completely alone in this world."

"But you aren't alone, Muse." He slowly turned around, my fingers gliding across his torso and then his stomach as he turned. He stopped once we were face-to-face, his head tilted toward me so he could look down at me. "You have me. You'll always have me."

I didn't overanalyze his words, knowing he meant them in a different context than I wanted. If I ever needed help, he would be there. All I ever had to do was call him, and he'd be by my side. He would be my friend for the rest of time, a protector that I never asked for. He was the only friend I had in the world—and he would always be my friend. "You know what I mean..." My hands started at his stomach and slowly glided up his chest. His pectoral muscles felt like a statue, so hard and smooth. "Tell me, Conway. Tell me why you're afraid."

He stared at me in intense silence. Time stretched on endlessly, and it didn't seem like he would say anything at all. His eyes gave nothing away, just his stern demeanor. He could stare for minutes without blinking, and his eyes never watered to protect the dry surface of his eyes. He wasn't bothered by the eye contact either.

Nothing knocked this man off-balance.

I kept waiting, kept hoping. He knew everything about me, every secret that I kept from the rest of the world. I trusted this man in a way I'd never trusted anyone before. I'd shared every piece of me with him.

I wanted some of him in return. "Conway."

He pulled his hands out of his pockets and grabbed my wrists. He held them gently as he stared down at me, the intensity in his gaze slowly softening. Then he pulled my hands away from my chest, lowering them back to my sides. He pulled his touch away entirely and crossed his arms over his chest. "I used to have an aunt. She died before I was born, before my parents got married."

Sadness overwhelmed me instantly. I knew he'd lost someone, judging by his mother's tone. But I suspected the way she died was worse than the death itself.

"She was taken by a ruthless arms dealer. Apparently, he had bad blood with my family. He tortured her and raped her...and my father and uncle did everything they could to get her back. They finally settled on a deal, an exchange of twenty million dollars. But the man, his name was Bones, didn't uphold his end of the deal. When my aunt was returned to my father, Bones shot her in the back of the head."

I covered my mouth to quiet my gasp.

"And kept the money. My father watched the light leave her eyes. He watched her fall to the concrete, and before her head hit the ground, she was dead. My father said he would never forget that moment for as long as he lived. It still visits him in his nightmares."

"Conway, I'm so sorry."

He wore the same expression as he did before, his look cold and guarded. "Her name was Vanessa."

I made the connection immediately. "They named your sister after her..."

He nodded. "My dad and uncle have never gotten over it...even though it's been thirty years. They're protective of my mother and aunt, hardly letting them out of their sights. And with Vanessa, it's even worse. She's so damn beautiful and so stubborn. She worries me. And now that I have you, I can't let anything happen to you. Seeing you stripped naked while some psychopath tried to buy you… I can't even think about it anymore." He lowered his gaze. "I'd never forgive myself if something happened to you. And my mom… She's a beautiful woman. Age hasn't broken her the way it has most people. If someone wants to attack my father or me, she's a prime target. So, yes, I'm extremely protective, overbearing, and paranoid. Don't expect me to change, because I never will."

I thought back to the woman he rescued from the Underground. He bought her and then handed her off to Carter so she could be returned to her family. Now it all made sense. "That's why you save those women? That's why you were at the Underground."

"Partially," he said. "I can't lie and say it's a totally selfless act. The Skull Kings purposely steal women from powerful men. They're commissioned by their enemies. Then those families come to us and pay us to get their daughters back. It's expensive, but Carter and I aren't going to risk our necks for free. Then we bid on them and return them to their families. It's an easy way to make money—and it helps people at the same time."

The fact that he made a profit off it didn't make me think less of him. He was still doing a noble thing. He could easily buy a woman to torture himself. Or he could capture women by the dozens and sell them on the black market. He didn't do that either. "I think you're brave. If they caught you..."

"I'm only brave for the money."

"I don't believe that. You're a billionaire, Conway. What does a few million more mean to you?"

"It's not just a few million. These families are paying us between ten and twenty million euros—tax-free."

"And if someone spotted you in there, it could ruin your reputation."

"I design lingerie. I don't have much of a reputation anyway."

"Yes, you do," I said. "You're a strong man who made his own way in life. You started from nothing in your industry and made yourself into something. You're generous and kind. I think you're a wonderful person."

His eyebrows arched before his eyes narrowed. Like I'd said the wrong thing, his expression turned into a glare. "I'm okay with being what I am, Muse. Like I told you before, I'm not evil—but I'm not good either. The second I had leverage over you, I made you into my prisoner. I didn't treat you with respect, and I took your virginity instead of letting you find the right guy. Let's not rewrite history. Let's not change my character."

I knew he meant every word because I could feel the sincerity in his words. I could see the seriousness in his eyes. He wasn't fishing for a compliment to counteract his statements. He just wanted to correct my assumption. "You were the right guy, Conway."

His glare slowly faded away, replaced by a deeper look.

"You gave me money when you didn't even know me so I wouldn't have to sleep on the street. When I left your company, you tried to give me more money and a phone. Then when I was about to be sold off to a monster who would do horrific things to me, you spent a fortune just to keep me safe. You've paid all my debts and set me free. You've given me a place to live, food to eat. Without you, I would be dead right now. We both know it. You saved my life, Conway. You've given me a chance to start over. You're the only man who has ever earned the right to have me...and I have no regrets."

His breathing deepened as his eyes narrowed on my face.

"No, you haven't been Prince Charming. But a white knight in shining armor is overrated. That's not what I want. I want you exactly as you are, all the good and all the bad. I accept you for who you are, Conway. But you need to learn to accept yourself too—that you're a great man."

When I woke up the following morning, Conway was gone.

I'd become lazier over the last few days, spending more time in the house and with Conway rather than outside in the blazing sun. So, when his alarm went off, I ignored it and stayed asleep.

I spotted the rose on the nightstand along with the note as I opened my eyes.

The rose was white, in full bloom and lovely. I held the flower to my nose and smelled it before reading the note.

Muse,

Join me in the studio.

Conway didn't sign it, but I could smell his scent on the paper. I quickly brushed my teeth and got ready before walking down the hall to where he spent his time working. He was standing at the table, working a fabric with his hands. A breakfast tray sat at the table, the lid placed over the food to keep it warm. A pot of coffee with steam rising from its opening was waiting for me.

"Morning."

He looked up from his work, his concentration shattered the second I spoke. He looked at me the same way he did anytime our eyes connected. Full of intense possessiveness, the warmth of his gaze could be felt across the room. He set down his tools then walked around the table to greet me. "Morning." His thick arms circled my waist, and he bent his neck down to kiss me. His kiss was soft but full of restrained aggression. If he didn't control himself, he'd probably crush my mouth with his excitement. Instead, he gripped me tighter than usual. His thumbs dug into my stomach, restricting my ability to breathe. There was a lot of lip and also touches of tongue. He breathed into my mouth, expanding my lungs with his masculine breath.

It was a great way to say good morning, to be cherished by this sexy man.

His hands slid down to my ass, and he squeezed my cheeks hard.

When he finally pulled away, I was so hard up that I didn't care about breakfast. And I was one of those people who really believed breakfast was the most important meal of the day. I bit my bottom lip when he turned back to the table, wanting more of that kiss along with something else.

He grabbed the lingerie he was working on, a gray one-piece that was cut along the waistline. It showed bare skin before it connected to the panties at the bottom. With a crotch that unfastened, it allowed easy access without having to take the garment off. "I want to see you in this." He walked over to me, feeling the silk fabric in his fingertips. There was a diamond pendant in the middle, another jewel that was more expensive than my mother's house, even in a seller's market.

Lady in Lingerie

It must have taken him a while to do this. He could never create something in less than three hours. His hands worked so much detail into his pieces, and he needed to construct every inch of clothing with expert hands. "How long have you been awake?"

"Since three."

"Couldn't sleep?" I took the lingerie from his hands, feeling the softness between my fingertips.

"Too inspired." He slid his hands into the pockets of his jeans.

As I looked down to stare at the lingerie again, I noticed the front of his pants. The outline of his big cock was noticeable, the bulge impressive. But it didn't do justice to what was waiting underneath. "Turn around."

He released a sigh of annoyance before he complied.

I removed the dress I wore and pulled on the gray lingerie. It was skintight around my bust, the strapless top fitting my measurements so well that it stayed up easily.

It was beautiful. So simple, but so perfect.

I didn't have any heels on, and there wasn't a pair in sight. Barefoot would have to do even though it wasn't the best choice. At least it was easier on my feet.

He turned around when he thought enough time had passed, and the second his eyes raked over me, his entire body tensed as all his muscles tightened collectively. His eyes showed his desire, and the way his fingers curled toward his palm showed the way he wanted to grab me.

Now I felt like prey.

And he was the ultimate predator.

This time, he didn't show any restraint. He moved into me and backed me into the wall, making my small body thud against the hardness. His hands snaked over my body, feeling the lingerie against my skin. He explored every inch, his face pressed to mine. He felt the curve of my hips then squeezed my tits with his large palms. A growl erupted in my face, the growl of an animal that wanted to sink his teeth into me.

He yanked his shirt over his head, pulling it from the back until his head popped through. All of his movements were sexy, even the way he rushed through undressing. He left his jeans on as he kissed me, his hands moving to my rib cage.

I kissed him back and undid the top button of his pants, feeling the incredible heat against my mouth. I couldn't believe there was ever a time when he didn't want to kiss me, that he'd taken something so incredible off the table. Now it was the thing I enjoyed most, the action that made me feel most connected to him.

I pushed his jeans and boxers down so his throbbing dick could come free. Throbbing and slightly red, he was drooling at the crown. My slickness would combine with his, and the combination of our two bodies would be utterly incredible.

His hand moved between my legs, and he unfastened my crotch. His fingers lingered behind, feeling the buildup of moisture coat his fingertips. "Fuck..." His lips moved to my ear, and he breathed into my canal as he fingered me, exploring my soaked cunt. When he fingered me for the very first time, he could only get a single finger inside. I was too tight, too innocent. Now I could take all of him with just a slight twinge of pain.

He lifted me against the wall and pinned my back in place as he tilted his hips to press his cock between my folds. His crown moved against my entrance before he shoved himself in, sliding down my wet channel until he was completely inside.

I gripped his shoulders and breathed next to his ear, feeling full from his enormous cock. "God..."

He pressed his face to mine as he remained deep inside me, his thick cock stretching me as wide as I could go. My body could barely accommodate him, but that fullness made the sex so good. I couldn't imagine being with another man, couldn't imagine having sex as good as this. Friends told me sex was hit or miss. Sometimes it was good, but most of the time, it wasn't. The guy usually cared more about finishing than getting the woman off. And some of my friends didn't like sex at all because it was never good.

That meant Conway was different.

Not just different because he was gorgeous, but different because he prided himself on his performance. He'd never fucked me without letting me finish first—except when he was trying to punish me for something.

He started to move, pressing me hard into the wall as he rocked his hips back and forth. He gripped my ass as he kept me suspended, his thick arms tightening and bulging with the beautiful muscles of his body. As if he'd picked me up in a bar and couldn't wait to take me home to fuck me, he gave it to me hard, right then and there. He didn't kiss me, but he looked into my face with every thrust, watching my reaction to him.

It felt so good to watch this sexy man hold me so effortlessly and fuck me at the same time. I loved watching him build up a sweat, loved staring at his naked body in the mirror on the other side of the room. He was over six feet of all man, tight muscles in his ass and his back. The muscles of his flank tightened and shifted as he worked his body to please me. When we were pressed together this closely, he ground right against my clit. The stimulation was over the top and powerful.

I could barely keep my eyes on him because my lids were becoming heavy, not with sleep but with arousal. Like a spell had been cast over me, my body relaxed, but it only calmed in preparation for the storm.

"Muse." He exhaled into my face, the sweat forming on his back and dripping all the way to his ass. He tightened his jaw as he breathed through his movements. "You." He thrust into me deep. "Are." He released a moan as he hit me in the perfect spot. "Mine."

Every time he claimed me, I felt my legs quiver. I wanted to be his. I loved the way he got jealous whenever a man looked at me for too long. I loved the way he stepped in front of me so that a man wouldn't kiss me on the cheek. I loved the way he didn't allow his models to touch him anymore because he knew it bothered me. I loved all the sacrifices he made to keep me, by kissing me, making love to me, setting me free, and committing to me.

It was more than he'd ever done for anyone else.

Now he was ramming me into the wall, giving me his big cock over and over again.

I pressed my face into his neck and clawed at his back while I watched him fuck me. His jeans had slid down to his ankles from his movements, and his tight ass looked so good as it worked, grinding into me. "Conway...yes." I breathed into his ear and closed my eyes, feeling my pussy tighten around him. I came with an explosion, squeezing his dick mercilessly. My nails were even worse, cutting into his back and nearly drawing blood.

Conway couldn't wait until I was finished. He gave his final pumps and came inside me, giving me his heavy seed as he groaned. He pressed me against the wall and shoved his dick as deep as he could, his ass tight from keeping me in place. He gave me so much seed that it already started to drip out of me and onto the floor.

Conway held me in place as he caught his breath, the sweat streaked across his body and probably burning the small wounds my nails had caused. Once he recovered from the wave of pleasure that had just exploded out of his balls, he carried me to the couch and sat back against the cushion, placing me on his lap. With a flushed face and sweat on his upper lip, he looked just as sexy as he did when he finished a workout. He pushed his body to the max to make me feel good, giving me everything he had because he cared about my climax as much as his own. His cock slightly softened inside me, and he massaged my thighs gently as he looked into my face.

My arms circled his neck, and I kissed him. "I like it when you fuck me like that."

"Like what?"

"Like you've never fucked me before." I sucked his bottom lip, giving it a gentle bite before releasing it.

His hands snaked up my body, feeling the silk that was now soaked with his sweat. It was tight on my chest and my waist, but it made me look more petite than I really was. That was the magic behind Conway's designs. He could make your most flattering feature even better.

"Is there time to get this ensemble into the show?"

He pressed kisses down my neck and to my collarbone, his tongue licking away the sweat that sprinkled across my body. "No." He rubbed his nose against mine. "I made this just for you."

He made me a piece of lingerie he'd never debuted before, like the white ensemble he made me wear when he took me for the first time. At the time, the gesture didn't seem special. I was scared and uncomfortable. But now, his actions meant something to me. They made me feel special, made me feel honored to wear something he created just for me. He only wanted me to wear it, so it was a one-of-a-kind piece from a genius designer.

And it was all mine.

"Thank you. That was sweet."

His hand dug into the fall of my hair, and he brought my lips toward his for a kiss. He kissed me softly, his lips taking me gently. His fingers fisted my hair, wrapping it around his knuckles like he was trying to anchor me against him. There was no need to tie me down when I never wanted to go anywhere else.

And he hardened inside me all over again.

"You're my woman," he whispered. "And my woman deserves something no other woman can ever have."

5
CONWAY

My driver placed the suitcases in the trunk and hung Muse's dresses in the back seat. We were being taken to the Milan airport where my plane was waiting for us. It was gassed up and ready to take us across the Atlantic to New York.

I didn't fly commercial—not even first class.

If I was ever out in public for too long, people asked for autographs and pictures. I didn't want to sound ungrateful, but where there was one person, a herd soon followed afterward. Then I was swarmed by people like a famous actor, and I wasn't in this business for sidewalk fame.

Muse and I sat in the back seat while my driver took us to the airport. Muse was in jeans and a t-shirt, a type of outfit she hadn't worn since the first time I'd met her. Now she wore my designer clothes because she only deserved the best. But since we were going to be on a nine-hour flight, she wanted to be comfortable.

Little did she know, she wouldn't be wearing anything on the flight.

We spent the drive in silence since my driver was in the front of the SUV. As time passed, I became even more possessive of my muse, of the inspiration for my creative design. She wasn't just my intellectual property, but the pussy I buried myself in every night. I didn't want another man to even hear the sound of her voice.

I wasn't sure how it had gotten this bad.

Muse looked at her phone for a few minutes before she set it aside and looked out the window.

Since she wasn't looking, I turned my gaze to her and watched her. I studied the way she watched the fields as they passed. Her thick eyelashes moved when she blinked, and her eyes reflected the golden sunlight that pierced through the tinted windows. Her legs were crossed, and her curled hair was pulled over one shoulder. Even dressed down in jeans and a t-shirt, she was still the sexiest woman I'd ever had.

My hand moved to her thigh.

She glanced at my fingers before she turned her gaze on me. Then she gave me a smile, the kind of smile that reached her eyes and made them light up a little brighter.

Maybe it was the golden sunlight or the backdrop behind her, but in that moment, she looked more beautiful than she did in any of my lingerie. She looked more beautiful than when she was buck naked on my bed.

Because none of that mattered.

She had her own special beauty, the kind no one else could compete with.

She turned away and looked out the window again.

But my gaze was focused on her completely. I wanted to stare at her like that forever—whether she was looking at me or not.

THE CAR PULLED ONTO THE RUNWAY BESIDE THE LARGE private jet that was waiting for me. The stairway was down, ready to take us onboard once we hopped out of the car. Muse looked at the large plane that could accommodate hundreds of people, her mouth open. "This is yours?"

"Yes."

"Seriously? You own a plane this big?"

I loved it when she was impressed with me. It was superficial, and for a man as secure as I, it was a stupid thing to care about.

But I wanted to impress this woman every chance I

got. "Yes."

"I've never been on a private plane before."

"I think you'll like it. There's a bed, a few showers, and a dining room."

Her eyes were filled with more excitement than I'd ever seen. "This is so amazing." She opened the door and got out just as the man opened the back and grabbed our bags to be carried onto the plane.

My phone rang. If my father's name weren't on the screen, I would have ignored it. "Father, how are you?"

"Good. Just wanted to see when you were leaving."

"I'm actually about to board the plane."

"Oh, I see. I wanted to wish you good luck. I'm sure your show will be great, but nonetheless, hope it goes well."

"Thanks. I think everyone will be impressed by the new line." Especially when the sexiest woman in the world had inspired every single design. All the other models despised Muse, but that was because they were jealous—jealous that they would never be as beautiful.

"Your mother told me she had a nice time with Sapphire. Seems to really like her."

"Yes, all of you have told me that you love the woman…" I was glad they liked her, but they shouldn't get too attached. I couldn't picture my life without Muse, but I knew this wouldn't last forever. At least, it wouldn't end in marriage and a family.

He chuckled. "I guess we're relieved that the one woman you want is good for you. I worry about your sister a lot, for obvious reasons. But I worry about you too, son. I want a woman who's perfect for you. And Sapphire seems perfect."

Now I regretted introducing her to them. They'd already included her in the family. I knew Muse treasured those relationships because she didn't have a family of her own. She loved my sister, and now she loved my parents. And they loved her just as much.

But it got me into deep shit. "I'm glad I have your approval."

"You don't need my approval, son. But I want you to know you have it. I'll see you when you get back. Your mother and I want to hear about the show."

"Of course. Talk to you later."

"Love you, Con."

My dad didn't normally say that when we were getting off the phone, so I knew he was worried about me being out of the country. I was the last person he needed to be concerned about. I had even more money than he did, and my security team were retired Navy SEALs. But at the end of the day, I was his son. "I love you too, Dad."

I boarded the plane, and the flight attendant shut the

door, locking it behind me. I moved to the seat beside Muse in the center of the plane, the seat I had to take until we were in the air. I buckled myself in and rested my ankle on the opposite knee, waiting for takeoff.

"This plane is beautiful," Muse said. "The bathroom… is like a regular bathroom. I've never seen that before. And the bedroom is so nice. If I could fly like this everywhere, I would travel across the world."

And I would love to take her around the world. "I'm glad you like it."

"Who were you on the phone with?" She didn't ask questions like that often, but I knew she was just making conversation.

If this were three months ago, I would have told her off for asking. Now, it didn't bother me. "My father."

"Is he coming to New York?"

"No. Too much work to do here."

The plane approached the runway and prepared for takeoff. "That's too bad. I was hoping to see them."

My parents loved her—and now she loved them. "He said my mom enjoyed seeing you the other day."

"She did?" she asked with a smile. "She's so nice. And easy to talk to."

I wasn't close to my mom the way I was with my father. But she'd been a great mom. I didn't have a single complaint. She was smart, elegant, and did a good job raising me. As I aged, I realized most people didn't have what I had—and I wasn't referring to money. "She's great."

"My mom was always difficult," she said. "Kinda distant with a hint of depression. She was never the same after my father died. And I wasn't close with him either. You're lucky your parents are so involved in your life."

I was a grown man, and my father still said he loved me. I pretended I didn't need to hear it, but when I felt warmth touch my soul when he showed his affection, I knew I did need to hear it. All I did was give her a nod because I wasn't sure what else to say.

The plane took off, cruising into the sky at exceptional speed. We leaned back, our weight shifting into the seats. We stayed like that for several minutes before the plane leveled off.

"I have a question."

I unbuckled my safety belt. "Alright."

"Why do you live in Verona? You're hardly at the office in Milan, so why don't you live closer to your parents?"

I'd bought that house after living in Milan for a few years. I'd started making serious money, and I wanted to live somewhere nice and close to work. That was almost ten years ago. "I started my career in Milan, so I didn't have much of a choice on where to live. It's the fashion capital of the world. I was working sixteen-hour days to make it big. Once money started to come in, I decided to buy a nice place outside the city—somewhere with peace and quiet. I didn't purchase the property with the intention of staying away from my parents."

"But now that you work from home most of the time, why don't you move back to Florence?"

The question was odd, and I suspected her curiosity had something to do with her lunch with my mom. "Why do you ask?"

"Your mother told me your parents wished you live closer."

My heart immediately throbbed in sadness. I hated disappointing them. I hated knowing they missed me.

"She said your father has never gotten used to the distance."

And now it felt like she'd stepped right on my heart.

"Maybe you should sell that place and buy something close to them," she suggested. "That seems like something you might enjoy."

"Did my mother ask you to say this?"

"No. But I think it would make both of you happy."

Returning to Tuscany sounded nice. I loved the heat and the mild winters. I would love to see my parents on a regular basis. After everything they did for me, I would love nothing more than to make them happy. "I can't move back right now, not when Vanessa is in Milan. She'd be there alone."

"Isn't Carter there?"

"I'm her brother," I said. "It's different."

"But you can't live your life based on Vanessa," she said. "She wouldn't want you to."

"The idea of her living in that big city alone while we're all five hours away makes me anxious. When she finishes school, I'll think about it again. I know she'll move back to Tuscany when she's done."

"You think?"

"Yeah. She wants to live on her own for a while because she needs her independence. But she's really close with my mom, and she loves being home every time we visit. When she moves back, I'll consider it."

"Great. Because I would love to live there too."

I stared straight ahead, but I felt my heart beat quicker in my chest. She spoke of our future together like it was certain, and that filled me with both joy and terror. If she were still living with me two years from now, the relationship would feel more serious. I'd already been with her longer than any other woman in my life. That would be a whole new kind of commitment. For a man not looking for love or marriage, that sounded like the very thing I was trying to avoid.

So, I forced myself to stop thinking about it.

Muse stretched out underneath the sheets, pointing her toes and bringing her arms above her head. A quiet moan escaped her lips, and her eyes fluttered open a moment later. "I've never slept so well on a plane before..."

I lay on my back with her beside me, my tablet held up so that I could look through my emails. Everything was set for the show, and the girls were already in New York. I went through the performance over and over in my mind, but there was nothing left to change. It was ready to go.

But I couldn't deny I was nervous.

Everyone questioned whether my best model would be in the show, and if she weren't, it would affect my work. But if she were on my arm for the evening, pulled into my side with affection in her eyes, that should still be good enough. She wasn't my model anymore because she was the woman in my bed.

The world would know I was the one fucking her.

She turned over and cuddled into my side, her arm draping over my waist and her cheek resting against my shoulder. "Did you sleep?"

"A little."

"Why are you nervous?"

"Never said I was." I set my tablet to the side, knowing

I wouldn't be able to read when she was in the mood to talk.

"I know. But I can tell you are." She propped herself up on her elbows and looked down at me. "I'm just not sure why. You have nothing to be nervous about, Conway. Those women are so proud to model for Barsetti Lingerie that they're going to give everything they have. And the designs you've created are absolutely beautiful. Any woman could wear them, and no one would deny how stunning they are."

I looked up into her face, seeing the softness in her eyes and the rosy color in her cheeks. Her brown hair was slightly messy, and it was pulled back from her face, showing off her incredible features. Makeup or no makeup, she was ready for the runway at any time.

She placed her palm against my chest and gave me a gentle rub. "So, don't worry about it."

"I'm not the kind that worries."

She couldn't stifle the laugh that flew out of her mouth. "Yeah, okay. You're the biggest worrier I know."

"Incorrect."

She rolled her eyes. "Whatever you say." She lay back again on the soft sheets. "This is the only way to travel."

"I'm glad you approve."

"I'm serious. I've never slept like that on a plane

before. They're always so uncomfortable, and there's always a baby crying somewhere…no offense to babies."

The attendant knocked on the door. "Mr. Barsetti, we'll be landing soon. Take a seat and buckle yourself in."

"Can we just stay here?" Muse pulled the sheets up and released a happy sigh.

"Unfortunately, no." I kissed her shoulder before I got out of bed. "But we can sleep on the way back."

"Yay." She pulled on her clothes and fixed her hair before we returned to the seats toward the front of the plane. The plane landed on the runway smoothly, and then we were escorted to my car that was waiting for us on the runway. The transfer was easy, and within minutes, we were in the heart of Manhattan.

Muse stared out the window and looked at the street corners and the shops that were along the road. Her gaze didn't change as she examined everything, and it was difficult to tell how she felt about being back in her hometown.

I watched her, noting every single time she blinked and pursed her lips. I'd give anything to know exactly what she was thinking at any given time. Her mind fascinated me. I wanted to know everything about her, even the unimportant details.

We arrived at the hotel and checked in at the front desk where we were escorted to the top floor where the presidential suite awaited. It was ten thousand square feet and much too big for two people, but I refused to accept anything less than the most expensive room in the hotel.

Muse looked around, her eyes scanning the chandelier hanging from the ceiling, the full kitchen, and the enormous living room that could house a hundred people. She walked along the floor-to-ceiling windows and admired the view while my men carried all her luggage inside. They handled her dresses with care before placing them in the closet. They were staying in the room across from me, so my security detail could watch the front door and monitor anyone who tried to reach this floor.

Muse stood at the windows with her arms crossed over her chest. The light had disappeared over the horizon, and now the darkness was blanketing the city. Neon lights were brighter, and the street lamps down below were more visible.

I stood behind her and stared at her, watching her petite form contrast against the backdrop of the biggest city in the world. I knew Muse in a different context, so it was difficult for me to imagine her living here. She fit in so much better in Verona, working her hands in the stables and being close to the earth. She complemented the quiet beauty of the landscape, almost like she was born and raised there.

I came up behind her and placed my hands on her hips.

She'd obviously been so focused on the view that she didn't hear my approach. She took in a deep breath, her waist tightening automatically.

My fingers stretched over her rib cage, feeling the muscles and tiny bones underneath. "Do you miss it?" The height of my head surpassed hers, so it was easy to look over at the city beyond. The glass was so clean that I could see her reflection, see the way her gaze shifted upward to look at me.

"I know this is going to sound strange but…not really."

My fingers tightened a little farther in response, loving that answer a lot more than I anticipated.

"I was born and raised here, so it has a special place in my heart. But it doesn't feel like home anymore. I like looking out the window in the morning and seeing the golden hillsides and the vineyards. I like smelling the dirt when I work in the stables. I like the wet heat that sticks to my skin and hearing the crickets and the birds. It's so peaceful. It's so quiet. Now, I'm surrounded by constant noise, by the pollution from all the taillights. The lights so bright. They never used to blind me, but now I can barely look at them. There're so many people on the sidewalk, people intent on getting to the next place as quickly as possible. Speed is constant, and time never slows down.

When I lived here, I was always on the go. If I wasn't doing something, I felt lazy. But in Italy, the culture is so different. Taking the time to appreciate the sky and the smell of the grass is important."

She described my world so perfectly, painting it into a lively picture I immediately recognized. She understood what I loved about it so much because she described it down to the very last detail. I'd seen a lot of beautiful places in my life, visited foreign countries with so much natural beauty it was difficult to process. But there was something about the Italian hillsides that brought me a sense of peace. "I know exactly what you mean."

She slowly turned around and looked up into my face. "Well, it's nine o' clock, but I slept on the plane all day. Not really tired. What should we do?"

My hands glided under her forearms, feeling the soft skin I loved to touch. "What would you like to do?"

"I'm hungry," she said. "Maybe we can order some dinner."

"Would you like to go out?"

"It's a Friday night. Everything will be booked."

I couldn't suppress the grin on my face. "Not for Conway Barsetti."

I didn't eat dinner this late, but for me, it was morning. We went to one of the nicest restaurants in Manhattan, and the second I met the host at the podium, he showed me to a table without even asking if I had a reservation.

Once again, Muse was impressed.

I liked impressing her. It gave me a sense of power I couldn't get anywhere else. With a billion dollars to my name and a garage full of expensive cars, I had enough wealth to impress a foreign prince. But I never cared what anyone thought of me. My sense of self-worth had always been untouchable. But I enjoyed watching the way her eyes lit up whenever she got to experience a hint of luxury. She acted like the plane was one of the coolest experiences she'd ever had. And now she took in my presidential suite, still stunned that I could afford this without making the slightest dent in my bank account.

And now she was impressed I could get her into any establishment without saying a single word.

I liked spoiling her, especially when she appreciated it. Most of the women expected to be spoiled, wanted to be treated to a fancy dinner so they could be seen in public with me. Muse was nothing like that. Money wasn't important to her the way it was to everyone else. She preferred a simple life, earning everything she was given.

And she definitely earned my affection every night.

She wore a black dress Dante had picked up from my favorite designer in Verona, skintight and flattering against her curves. Her hair was done and makeup was plastered on her face, looking like she hadn't just spent nine hours on a plane. She held the menu open and looked at the selections.

I'd already ordered the wine, the thing I cared most about, so I stared at her instead. I studied the thickness of her eyelashes, the way her lipstick contrasted against the paleness of her face. This was my hundredth time looking at her, but I never got tired of it. I never knew when a rush of inspiration would hit me. With her, it could happen at any moment.

"I'll take the New York strip," she said. "Medium well. And can I have some broccoli on the side?"

"Of course." The waiter wrote down her order then turned to me.

"I'll have the same thing." I handed the menu over.

"Good choice, sir." He left us alone at the table, a table in the corner right next to the window. A white tablecloth was on top, along with a single white candle in the center and our bottle of wine. There was more space around us than the rest of the tables, probably denoting it as a special VIP area. It was no coincidence it was right against the windows, so paparazzi and anyone with a phone could snap a few pictures.

She swirled her wine then took a drink, treating her glass like an expert wine taster. Spending time around my business and my lifestyle had given her new skills. She knew a lot about wine, about the differences in color and taste. She knew how to pair it with meals and could even distinguish the gentle characteristics in the flavor, like oak, fruit, and other additives.

She was becoming a very refined woman.

My favorite thing of all was her silence. She could sit across from me for thirty minutes straight without saying a single word. There was no necessity to fill the silence with pointless conversation. Other people were uncomfortable with my tense quietness, but she didn't seem to mind.

She looked out the window as she kept her fingers on the stem. Her nails were painted, and a natural tan bronzed her skin. Her hair had been cut, and she was groomed for the show tomorrow night even though she wouldn't be performing. But this was the first time I would ever bring a woman with me as a date. I always showed up to my shows alone. There was never a woman in my life who earned the luxury.

But Muse certainly did.

I wanted the world to know she was too busy being mine to model.

She turned back to me and gave me a soft smile from across the table.

I felt the muscles of my stomach harden in response. Such simple gestures had a grand effect on me. She had more power than she realized—and I hoped she never realized it.

"Can I ask you something?"

"Yes."

"So, Carter is a car guy, right?"

"Yes." My forearms tightened when she asked about another man. Carter was my family, but he still had the Barsetti blood that drove women crazy. He was handsome, landing as many women as I could.

"And he designs luxury cars and produces them? That's so crazy. I don't understand how somebody would even start that kind of business. It seems like there are distinctive brands of cars all over the world, but they've been around for a long time. How do you start something new?"

"By working your ass off and offering something other competitors can't."

"What does Carter offer? What's different about his cars?"

"The sleek design. The aerodynamics. But he's also made a luxury car that has the lowest gas emissions of any other vehicle. And more importantly, he's the first person to release an electric car with the same power as a V12 engine. Competitors are still trying to figure out how he did it."

"How did he do it?"

The corner of my mouth rose in a smile. "Like he would ever tell me."

"Aren't you guys best friends?"

I was about to take a drink of my wine but changed my mind. "No. Men don't have best friends."

"Then what is he to you?"

I shrugged. "He's Carter."

She rolled her eyes. "You guys don't talk about business? I thought that's all you ever did."

"We do—but our business."

"Purchasing kidnapped women?"

I nodded. "We split it fifty-fifty."

"What's his role in this?"

"He has the connections. Families get in contact with him once their daughters or wives are taken. He handles the wire transfer and then tells me to head to the Underground."

"Why does he send you and not someone else?"

"I have a preexisting relationship with the Skull Kings. I also have a legitimate alibi. When I buy a woman, I usually put her in a show or an event one time. That way they think I'm using them for my own business gains. Then I release them, and by that time, the Skull Kings have moved on to something else and aren't paying attention to me anymore."

"What happens if they catch you?"

I took a long drink of my wine. "I won't be allowed back to the Underground. But I'm not sure if they would do anything more extensive. Technically, I'm not breaking any rules. I pay for my women fairly by winning the bid. What I do with them after that is none of their concern. When government officials have asked for my cooperation in taking down the Skull Kings, I always refuse. I won't rat on them. Therefore, there should not be repercussions in the event I'm caught."

"But if you never take down the Skull Kings, they'll just keep doing it. And you buy one woman, but what about all the others?"

My eyes narrowed. "I told you I wasn't a good man, Muse." Sometimes it bothered me that I did nothing, and those women were sent to their deaths. Sometimes it ruined my sleep. But other times, I didn't care at all. "Even if I eradicated their organization, someone else would just take over the business. People think crime can be snuffed out, but it can't. You take down one villain, but another villain always replaces them. That's just how it is."

Muse watched me from across the table without judgment in her eyes. Her features didn't show any particular feeling. She just sat there, her fingers resting on the stem of her glass.

"You think less of me." I shouldn't care about her opinion, but I did. It meant more to me than it should.

"No."

"Then what do you think?"

She released her glass and brought her hands to her lap. "I think there are a lot of shitty people in the world. They do horrific things. And the kind of evil they show is so intense that it makes your crimes pale in comparison. So, no, I don't think less of you, Conway. I wouldn't make love to you every night if I felt otherwise."

Make love. She made love to me.

I wanted to say we were just fucking, but I wouldn't always be on top if that were the case. My favorite position was having a woman on all fours, her ass in my face. I didn't want to look into her eyes. I didn't care about a deeper connection. All I cared about was a good fuck, getting my dick inside her at the perfect angle. But with Muse, I loved feeling her ankles lock together against my back. I loved feeling her heels dig into my ass. I loved looking into her eyes, watching her enjoy me, and I loved kissing her as I rocked into her slowly.

She was right. It wasn't fucking.

I slept with her every night. I had dinner with her every evening. She was such a large component of my life that it was hard to imagine not having her around. Without even realizing it, I'd become intensely attached to this woman.

The waiter brought our entrees, and we started to eat. Once our utensils were in our hands, we didn't spend time talking, but we returned to comfortable silence with the exchange of looks across the table.

I watched her enjoy her meal and sip her wine. I watched the way her hands handled her silverware. With perfectly straight posture and graceful movements, she was every bit the supermodel I'd trained her to be.

But I'd also trained her to be the perfect woman.

WHEN MUSE STEPPED OUT OF THE BATHROOM, SHE WAS dressed in a white ensemble I'd created just for her. In a push-up bra lined with diamonds and a white thong that complemented her tanned skin perfectly, she was gorgeous.

I sat against the headboard and watched her enter the bedroom. With an hourglass figure and long legs, she was gorgeous from head to toe. My cock was hard the second she walked into the bathroom with the racy pieces in hand. I didn't need to see her to know she would look stunning.

My memory was good enough.

She sauntered into the room, her eyes locked on me. This time, she wore heels, silver pumps that matched her diamonds. She stood at the foot of the bed and ran her fingers through her hair.

My fantasy.

I grabbed my phone, which was hooked up to the sound system, and I turned on music from a playlist. "Strip for me."

She hesitated, her confidence waning.

One hand circled my length under the sheets, and I brushed my thumb across the hardness of my dick.

She swayed her hips from side to side then slowly peeled off the bra. It was three in the morning, and neither one of us was tired enough to go to bed. She unclasped the back and let it fall to the floor.

With hard nipples and a tint of pink across her chest, her tits were unbelievable. She didn't have a big rack, but I preferred small tits as long as they were proportional. When they were perky and firm like that, it was hard not to fall under a cloud of obsession.

Her hands moved down to her panties, and she slowly peeled those off. They moved to her ankles before she pushed them away.

"Touch yourself."

She faltered at that command too, even more

uncomfortable by the suggestion than when I asked her to strip.

"Touch. Yourself."

She continued to sway to the music before she placed her fingers between her legs. She circled her clit exactly the way I did to her. For the first minute, her breathing didn't change, and neither did her expression. But once she allowed herself to enjoy it, she finally relaxed and panted with her movements.

I jerked myself under the sheets, my hand moving slowly so I wouldn't blow my load sooner than I wanted. Seeing her in that white lingerie made me think of the night I claimed her innocence. It felt so good to break her in, to watch her cry because my dick was too big. I wanted to do that again. "Lie on the bed."

She pulled her hand away reluctantly before she crawled onto the bed.

"On your back."

She turned over, her ass eyes hanging over the edge.

I got out of bed, my hard dick hanging out because it was swollen with an immense amount of blood. I was hard-up from watching her touch herself, but I was even more aroused by what I was going to do.

I grabbed a bottle from my bag then stood at the foot of the bed. I placed her feet against my chest and let my throbbing dick lay against her wet folds. Slickness was seeping from her slit because her fingertips had stimulated her so deeply.

I separated her knees and leaned over her so I could kiss her.

She was anxious for my mouth. Her fingers dug into my hair, and she kissed me like it'd been too long since she had me. She gave me her tongue first, her excitement overpowering mine. "Conway..." She locked her ankles together at my back and tugged on me, wanting me right in that moment.

My cock twitched in anticipation before I pressed my cock down and slid it into her drenched pussy.

"Yes..." She pulled me into her deeper, moaning directly into my throat.

I moaned at her enthusiasm. "Want my cock, Muse?"

"Please."

I rocked into her hard, slamming my big dick deep inside her. I hit her again and again, stretching her wide apart while her pussy fought against me to tighten. I sucked on my forefinger and got it soaked before I pressed it against her back entrance.

Her asshole was tight, and the second she felt me, she tightened even more. Her moans faltered, and she stopped gripping me as her concentration was broken. "Conway, what are you—"

"I'm fucking you in the ass tonight." I pushed my finger

inside her and finally made my way inside. She was tighter, a million times tighter than her pussy. I pulsed my finger slowly, giving her body time to acclimate.

She didn't rock back onto my dick because she was too busy staring at my face. "I've never done that before."

"I know." That was why I was so excited for it. I moved my mouth to hers and kissed her so she would stop thinking about what my finger was doing. I fingered her harder as I fucked her pussy. My tongue danced with hers, and I felt her whimper against my lips from time to time. I pushed another finger inside, and I felt her stretch even more.

"Conway." She spoke against my mouth. "Even now, I struggle to take you. I don't think I can do it."

"You will."

The arousal was still in her eyes, but so was the uncertainty. She looked into my gaze and dug her nails into my chest. "You're so big, Conway..."

I closed my eyes and groaned, loving the way she said those words. This was my fantasy, listening to this beautiful woman compliment the size of my dick. She knew it would hurt, and that turned me on even more. "It'll hurt. You'll cry. But I'll be gentle with you." I looked into her eyes as I rammed my cock inside her, my fingers still working her ass. "And it'll feel good too."

"Do I have a choice?" she whispered.

The asshole inside me wanted to say this was happening whether she wanted it or not. But I wasn't the same man I used to be. I'd parted with my old ways over the last four months. I did more for her than I did for any other woman. I respected her when others couldn't earn that respect. "You always have a choice, Muse." If she said no, I would stop. But I didn't want to stop.

She stared at me as she considered her response, the desire in her eyes, along with the obvious hesitation. "Okay."

"Just tell me to stop." I thrust into her again and resumed my kiss. My embraces were soft and sensual, giving her my tongue and taking hers in return. My fingers still explored her ass, and I felt my dick thicken even more when I understood just how tight she was. I was taking another piece of her, having her in a way I never had before. The evil man inside me loved the sound of her tears, loved knowing she was fighting the pain as she enjoyed the pleasure.

When I felt like she was about to come around my dick, I pulled out and pointed my crown at her back entrance.

She immediately tensed, holding her breath.

"Relax." I kissed her again, my mouth forcing hers to cooperate. If she just trusted me, she would loosen up, and it would feel so much better.

She started to relax again.

I squirted the lube all over my dick then pushed inside her, getting my crown inside her tight little asshole. There was so much resistance, but that only made it better. It felt so fucking good, so tight and warm. I pushed inside more, slowly inching deep inside.

Her nails cut into my chest, and she panted against my mouth. Winces and moans came from her lips as she felt me slip inside.

I kept going, getting half my length inside her.

Now she was breathing hard, clawing at me like she didn't know what else to do.

I closed my eyes and rested my forehead against hers. "Fuck...so good." I let her squeeze me tightly, the lube doing its job to make the friction less unbearable. Then I held myself on both arms and started to thrust, getting inside her deep and slow.

She gripped my biceps and lay back, her tits shaking with every thrust I made. Her legs were spread wide apart, the backs of her knees locked in place by my arms. She moaned with the movements, wincing when my dick moved deep inside her.

I fucked her ass and claimed it as mine. My breaths were just as deep and labored as hers because it felt so damn good. She was so tight, so inexperienced. I moved a little deeper when she got used to it, sheathing more of my dick.

That's when the tears started. They welled up at the corners of her lids then streaked down her cheeks.

It turned me on just like last time, seeing her fight for control over the pain. But it also made me feel like shit at the same time. I shouldn't enjoy those tears, and I shouldn't be the one causing them. "You want me to stop, Muse?" I paused so I could kiss her tears away, letting them absorb on my lips.

She breathed against my face, her tears in her voice. "No. It feels good. It just also really hurts."

I started to move again, listening to her tears fill the bedroom. They kept streaking down her cheeks, but she never sobbed. Her ass started to loosen around me once she got used to it. Her nails clawed at my back, leaving marks and a little blood.

"Touch yourself." I guided her hand between her legs and rubbed her fingers over her throbbing clit.

Her moans immediately changed, becoming deeper while the tears kept coming.

Now I could barely stop myself from exploding. I wanted my come to sit inside her ass all night long. I wanted to feel that powerful orgasm that was about to rock my entire body. I knew it was going to be good. I could feel it approaching hard and fast.

But thankfully, she came first. She came with a scream that was louder than any other she'd made. Her nails sliced me, and her asshole tightened all around me. Her head rolled back, and her mouth remained wide open as she kept yelling directly into my face.

I came inside her as I watched her performance, getting off to everything I was seeing and feeling. I dumped all of my seed inside her, filling her tight little asshole with all my arousal. I wanted her to be full of me in every way possible. I wanted to fuck every little hole and make her mine completely.

I groaned against her neck as I finished. My cock slowly softened as I stayed inside her. My wounds burned as the sweat poured directly into them, and I listened to her breaths slowly decrease while mine did the same.

I lifted myself to look directly down at her, seeing that the tears were long gone. "How did that feel?"

"It hurt, but I came harder than I ever have. Not sure how that worked..."

"It's because I know what I'm doing." I kissed the corner of her mouth then slowly pulled out of her. Then I lifted her from the bed and carried her into the walk-in shower in the bathroom. The warm water filled the bathroom with steam, and her fancy makeup and hair spray were washed away with the running water.

Her mascara streaked down her face, and like she

knew it was there, she wiped it away with both hands. Staring down at her fingertips, she looked at the black ink before rubbing them together to dissolve the color.

Her eyes weren't red from her tears, and now that we were finished, she was back to her usual self. But she seemed tired, despite all the energy she had just fifteen minutes ago. She tilted her head under the water and let it streak down her body, the warmth enveloping her. She released a quiet sigh, so quiet I couldn't hear it. But when I watched her chest rise and fall, I knew it occurred.

Now that her makeup was gone, it was just her underneath the water. Beautiful skin, gorgeous eyes, and utter perfection.

I moved under the water with her and cupped her face, my fingertips touching her wet skin. My nose brushed against hers as I felt the warm water run down my back. Then I pulled her into me and kissed her.

Kissed her slowly.

When I had something this pretty, I wanted to cherish it. I wanted to enjoy it as much as possible, like it could be taken away from me at any time. Now that I'd given her freedom, she could walk away from me whenever she wanted.

But when I really thought about it, I wondered if I could keep my word if she really did leave.

What if she decided to stay in New York once the

show was over? Would I really be able to board my jet and leave? Would I really be able to say goodbye? She was such an integral part of my life that I couldn't imagine it.

I didn't want marriage and kids with this woman, but it seemed like I still wanted a lifetime.

It didn't make any sense.

I continued to kiss her under the water, to taste the shower on her lips. My hand cradled the back of her hair, and I felt my cock slowly harden once more. Arousal was natural when I kissed a woman like this, but sex wasn't my end game. I'd just had an amazing climax, had fucked my fantasy in the ass and watched her cry. The last thing I needed was more sex.

Now I just wanted her.

I wanted this connection between us, this intimacy. Her kiss was the luxury I lived for, something that made me weak in the knees. When I was with her, I felt like a teenager all over again. I felt the heat in my stomach and the excitement in my lungs every time I took a breath. I'd bedded so many women before her, all perfect in their own ways.

But there was something about this one…

Something about Muse.

I couldn't put my finger on it.

I broke away and grabbed the loofah sitting on the shelf. I drenched it in water before I squirted soap onto her chest. Then I started to scrub her, to wash away all the lube and oil that made its way everywhere. I massaged her skin, working the muscles that ached from her constantly perfect posture. I watched her eyes soften as I made her feel good, washed her clean after how dirty I'd just made her.

She watched me through her thick lashes, a faint smile on her lips. She softened directly at my touch, her body relaxing the longer I caressed her. She watched my hands and stared at the soap suds that started to cover her body. "Conway?"

"Yes?" I rubbed the sponge through the valley between her breasts and down her stomach.

"How many women have you been with?"

My sponge stopped at her hip, the suds running down her leg toward the drain. I kept my eyes on my movements before I lifted my gaze back to hers. She'd never asked me a question like that before, and it was probably because she never had the power to do so. "Why?"

"I'm just curious. You know about my past."

"You mean, your lack of a past."

"Whatever," she said. "I'm not asking as some jealous girlfriend."

Girlfriend. There was that word again. But I let it go. "I'm not sure, but several dozen."

"Several dozen?" she asked. "That's very vague."

"Well, I don't count every single conquest. I'd say it's less than a hundred, but barely."

She didn't show any reaction, keeping her thoughts to herself. "Have you ever done what we just did with any of them?"

I didn't spare her feelings. "Yes. There's nothing I haven't done."

"Can I ask you something else?"

I was letting her ask whatever she wanted, and that wasn't like me. I was a mysterious man, and I was protective of my privacy. I didn't share my thoughts or feelings. I'd never had a meaningful relationship with a woman in my entire life. They were just flings, one-night stands. But Muse had become my woman, my friend. "Yes." I forced the answer out because I thought she deserved a response. I thought she deserved more than just being coldly shut down.

She pressed her lips together tightly, taking her time before she worded her question. "Have I meant more to you than all the others? Or do you just see me as...a good lay?"

I was surprised she needed to ask the question at all. I thought the answer was staring at her right in the face. "I've never had another woman live with me before. I've never been monogamous with one woman, and that was by choice. I've never brought a date to one of my shows. In fact, I've never been photographed with a woman romantically. You've met my family, been in their home, and now you're here with me. Not to mention, I'm out a hundred million dollars because of you. So, if you have to wonder if you mean something to me, don't. Because you do."

6

SAPPHIRE

We sat in the backseat of the limo as we moved through the streets I used to walk down every afternoon. The bar where I used to work was just a few blocks away, and I walked to my house after work every single night. I never took a cab because I needed to pinch every penny I had.

Now I was sitting in a limo—Conway Barsetti beside me.

His knees were apart, and his hands rested in his lap. He wore black on black, his collared shirt matching his sleek jacket. His vest had three gleaming buttons, and his shiny watch contrasted against the dark colors he wore. He'd shaved that morning, so his jaw was clean, making the hard lines of his face more noticeable.

He was perfectly calm, like he wasn't about to step foot

into a crowd of photographers. He'd been quiet all day, spending time in a different room to handle all his phone calls and emails.

I was left to entertain myself.

The limo turned right at the light, heading toward the auditorium where the show was being held. Conway pulled out his phone, checked the screen, and then slipped it back into his pocket.

I moved my hand to his on his thigh, my fingers resting across the veins of his knuckles. I could feel his pulse, which was steady and slow. He was warm too, like always.

His eyes shifted to me.

I held his look then smiled. "You look really handsome, Conway."

His expression didn't change, his gaze hard and piercing. It didn't seem like he was going to say anything, not when his gaze was that intense. Then he turned his hand over and wrapped his fingers around my palm. "You outshine me, Muse. You outshine everyone."

The limo pulled up to the sidewalk, and waiting outside was a sea of reporters and photographers. People were filing into the auditorium, each dressed in their best dresses and suits. They must be fashion gurus.

We stopped at the curb but didn't get out.

I looked to him, waiting for an explanation.

He spoke quietly. "If you're important, people will wait."

Thirty seconds later, the driver came to the back and opened my door. The sound had been confined outside the car when the door was shut, but now that it was open, I could hear the screams from frantic girls. I could hear reporters immediately shouting out questions. The driver gave me his hand and helped me step out without stepping on my dress.

Conway had given me a beautiful gown, deep purple with a high slit in the side. With a sweetheart top, it was simple, showing lots of skin without any diamonds or rhinestones. My hair was down, my deep brown curls hanging loose. A diamond necklace hung around my throat, and a bracelet decorated my wrist. Everything I was wearing was more expensive than a dozen cars. I hardly felt worthy to wear such luxurious things. I thought I would get used to it by now, but I knew I never would.

Conway came next. And when he did, the lines of people on the street immediately cheered, screaming for him like he was a movie star. He stood upright, tall and proud, his shoulders broad and powerful. He flattened the front of his suit and didn't flash a smile to the crowd. Instead, he wore his usual intense gaze, a smolder that made every woman wish he was hers.

But he was mine.

Lights went off as the cameras flashed. Reporters tried to move in to stick a microphone in his face.

Conway grabbed my hand and pulled me with him, guiding me down the red carpet to the entryway. He kept me close, taking the lead as he pulled me past the crowd of people who reached over the rail to touch us.

One reporter managed to sneak into our path. "Mr. Barsetti, this is the first time you've been accompanied by a date. Is it safe to assume that Miss Sapphire is more than just your model?"

I was surprised by the personal question, especially because of the way the camera was shoved into his face. Every reporter wanted to get the best response from Conway, and they were willing to do anything to get it.

But Conway handled the situation calmly. "Yes. It's safe to assume." Then he pulled me inside.

Once we were inside the auditorium, the flashes finally stopped, but Conway was swarmed by another set of people. Editors, designers, and other industry professionals inundated him with greetings and questions.

I stood beside him, smiling and standing perfectly upright.

Some people ignored me.

Others instantly recognized me. Joan Ivory, the editor for an American fashion magazine, seemed more interested in me than him. "You're quite the star. You really make everything you wear stand out. This dress..." She looked down at it. "It's gorgeous."

"Thank you," I said.

"Does that mean you won't be on stage tonight?" she asked.

"No," Conway answered for me. "She's here as my guest."

"I see." Joan smiled. "I'm looking forward to the show. I have no doubt it'll be spectacular."

We moved farther inside, talking with more people as we walked. We came across an eccentric woman, dressed in a fur scarf and a jean dress. Her hair was large and poufy, and the pink glasses on her nose were shaped oddly. "Conway."

He greeted her with a handshake. "Israel, I'm glad to see you here."

I noticed the way he shook everyone's hand. Not once did he kiss a woman on the cheek. He didn't even hug anyone.

"I'm very excited to be here," she said. "I'm sure I'll be ordering in bulk." She turned to me. "I'm Israel. You're Sapphire, I remember you."

"Yes," Conway said. "She's my girlfriend."

She didn't do anything more than smile, but a knowing look came into her eyes. "It's nice to see you happy, Conway. And it's nice to see your work soar to new heights." She shook my hand before she walked away.

Hearing him call me his girlfriend sent a jolt of joy through my body. I asked him to label me that way, but I didn't think he would actually do it unless he had to.

With his arm around my waist, he guided me farther into the auditorium where the seats were. His security team trailed behind us, ready to intervene if they had to. But everyone kept a respectful distance, honoring the enormous presence he cast in the room.

He took to his row and guided me to my seat. He sat beside me, taking the chair next to the aisle. Once we were seated, no one bothered him again. His security team surrounded us, taking seats in the nearby chairs so he was cushioned with protection.

But it didn't seem like he needed it.

Perhaps he did it just so people wouldn't approach him. He must have spoken to a hundred people already—and the show hadn't even started.

His grabbed my hand and held it on my thigh, his fingers warm and his pulse soft. He sat upright in the chair, keeping his masculine posture despite the fact that the cushions were easy to sink into. He stared at the stage as his thumb brushed over my hand.

My head was slightly turned as I watched him. "You don't like to sit with people?"

He turned his gaze my way, the same smoldering and intense expression he'd been wearing all night still plastered on his face. Like he was a model himself, he projected a particular image. He was sexy like all the women in his lineup, but he didn't need to be half naked to be desirable. "No."

"Because?"

"They talk too much. I want to watch the show, uninterrupted."

"Well, I talk a lot."

His thumb continued to glide over my skin. "Yes, but I actually enjoy your company."

A smile automatically stretched across my lips. "I knew it."

The corner of his mouth rose in a smile. "Don't let it go to your head."

"Already has."

He leaned into me and kissed me, the embrace soft but long. It was PG-13, but I still felt the heat burn throughout all the veins in my body. His lips were soft, and his chin was smooth from his fresh shave.

I closed my eyes and enjoyed his affection, excited to get back to the hotel room so this kiss could turn into something more. I loved it when he was gentle like this, enjoying the connection between us rather than the pleasure of the flesh.

He ended the embrace and rested his forehead against mine, and that was even better than the kiss he'd just given me. I loved having a piece of him that no one else ever could. I loved sharing my life with him, being the recipient of his adoration and his lust. Andrew Lexington had put an incredible offer on the table, and while I struggled to say no, I was glad I did. You couldn't put a price on what I had with Conway. He said he didn't want anything more than what we had, but he'd made so many sacrifices for me already.

Maybe he would make those sacrifices too…when he was ready.

He turned away and faced the stage again, his hand giving mine a good squeeze.

The lights turned down low, and the show started.

CONWAY RECEIVED A STANDING OVATION WHEN THE show was over. The models lined the stage with their hands held together, fake performance smiles plastered across their faces. Everyone clapped and cheered.

Conway and I were the only ones who remained seated.

He stared at the stage with his same intense expression, not giving a single thought away. Whether he was the center of attention or not, he kept the same cool composure. Nothing rattled this man.

Then the models pivoted to him and beckoned him to stand.

The sound of applause intensified.

Conway wore a slight smirk then rose to his feet.

The cheering grew louder, and the models clapped for him. Then together, they gave a swift bow in his direction.

The sound was so loud I couldn't hear my own breathing. Everyone in the auditorium was standing and clapping for him, admiring a man for his commitment to creative genius. He said he didn't need me on the stage to prove he was a master at his craft.

And he was right.

He proved everyone wrong.

The applause finally died away, and people began to exit the auditorium.

His arm moved around my waist, and he pulled me into his side. "Now here comes the worst part."

"What's the worst part?"

"Talking."

My face was pressed close to his as we waited for our turn to step in the aisle. "Well, when we get back to the room, there won't be talking there…" My hand pressed against his chest, the same affection I showed him whenever we were in bed together. It conveyed my thoughts, conveyed the things I wanted to do but couldn't.

His gaze intensified, turning to a gentle smolder.

I tugged on the front of his jacket and directed his lips to mine, giving him a soft kiss while my eyes remained locked with his.

He kissed me back, watching my eyes with the same intensity. His hand tightened at my lower back, bunching the fabric of my dress together. I could feel his desire in his simple movements, feel the arousal between his legs without actually pressing against him.

He abruptly turned away and guided me down the aisle, like he was turning off his feelings on purpose. He kept his arm securely wrapped around my waist and guided me into the lobby. As he predicted, he was swarmed with questions.

Just as I would on stage, I presented myself with a smile. I watched Conway answer all the questions thrown his way with refined patience, and I pressed against him as he held me close. His eloquent answers were interesting to me, and not once did he give the impression that he didn't want to be there.

He was a good liar.

The talking continued for the next few hours. My heels were killing me, and my dress was so tight against my stomach. My bladder was full of the wine we'd drunk earlier, and I needed a moment to relieve myself. "I need to powder my nose, Conway."

He eyed me with disappointment before he let me go.

I walked across the lobby toward the stairs when a man with a microphone pointed straight at my mouth intercepted me. Another man holding a camera was right behind him as he blocked my way to the restroom.

I wouldn't be annoyed if I didn't have to pee so badly.

"Sapphire, what did you think of the show?"

"It was beautiful," I answered. "Conway is a genius. He proves it time and time again. Excuse me." I tried to step away.

But he blocked my path once again. "Is it true that you're the inspiration for all his designs? That you're no longer on the runway because you're working with him more privately?"

I had no idea where he got that information, and I had no idea if I should confirm it or deny it. No wonder Conway hated this part of his job. "An artist draws his inspiration from everything. There's no way to tell exactly where it comes from."

As if he anticipated my movements, the man moved in front of me again, continuing to hold the microphone in front of me. "Conway Barsetti has never taken a date to any of his shows before, and he's never been photographed showing affection with any woman. Is it safe to say that he's found love in you?"

Far too personal of a question, but since Conway was famous, people thought they had the right to ask whatever they wanted. It annoyed me, but I was more annoyed that I couldn't just say yes. "Please excuse me, sir. These heels may look beautiful, but they're deadly." I darted past him, and this time, I didn't slow down. Even when he moved in front of me again, I pretty much sprinted into the bathroom.

And finally found some damn peace and quiet.

Once we were in the back seat of the limo and the doors were shut, I could finally hear myself think. People converged on the sidewalk to watch Conway drive away. The reporters were still there, along with the other fashion icons who wanted another chance to speak with him. His models joined the throng in the lingerie they'd modeled on stage, and they came to the curb to watch him drive away.

Conway immediately relaxed the second the limo pulled away. He didn't even look out the window to watch his admirers disappear. He stared straight ahead, anxious to move forward.

"You outdid yourself this time, Conway."

He slowly turned his head toward me. "We'll know for sure once Nicole gives me the numbers."

"But I think it's a safe bet."

"Probably," he said quietly.

"And you didn't need me on that stage." There may be something about me that people found fascinating, but without his lingerie, I was just a woman. His creative designs spoke for themselves. The models were important, but they weren't everything.

"But I needed you beside me." He grabbed my hand and rested it on his strong thigh.

Hand-holding was something we didn't do until recently. Now, whenever we were in the car, his hand was on mine. Even when we were in public, it was something we did. But never before had he extended that kind of affection. Even when we drove to his house in Verona for the first time and I was terrified after my evening at the Underground, he didn't console me with affection.

But now, it was a regular aspect of our relationship.

I scooted to his side of the limo and rested my head on his shoulder. My arm encircled his waist, and I closed my eyes as his comfort washed over me. Although he was hard, he was the perfect pillow. He was warm and smelled like the man I slept beside every night.

His arm moved around my shoulders, and he pulled

me closer to him. It was three in the morning, and we were both tired from the long night, and jet lag was starting to set in. He brushed his lips against my hairline, his affection blanketing me once more.

Fifteen minutes later, we arrived at the hotel and took the elevator to the top floor. The second we were inside, I kicked off my heels and vowed never to wear them again, at least for such a long period of time. I didn't care how beautiful they were—they were torture.

I stepped inside our bedroom and let the dress fall into a pile on the floor. It was too beautiful to let wrinkle, so despite my exhaustion, I picked it up and placed it on a hanger.

Conway didn't feel the same way about his clothes. He dropped his jacket and tie on the floor, and then the rest of his clothes followed suit. Everything except his boxers ended up on the floor before he climbed into bed.

I pulled back the sheets and snuggled beside him, tired from the long night. My face hurt from smiling so much.

The lights were turned off, and we were surrounded by silent darkness.

Conway wrapped his powerful arms around me and cuddled me. Heat burst from his body, keeping me warm and comfortable. My eyes were so heavy that I could barely keep them open. After a while, I stopped fighting the fatigue.

But I knew Conway would want sex—because he always wanted sex.

I forced myself to sit up and maneuver on top of him.

His intense gaze darkened before he rolled me to my backside. "You're tired."

"So?"

He separated my thighs with his and held himself on top of me. We were close together, nearly one person. "Then let me do all the work."

"We always do it like this..." I knew he preferred hard fucking, when he pounded into me from behind. He got off to the sight of my tears, to the confession of my lack of experience. I knew he wanted more, and after having such a successful night, I assumed he would want something like that now.

He pressed his thick crown inside me and slid all the way inside, hitting me until his balls tapped against my ass.

My fingers immediately dug into his arms as I inhaled sharply through my teeth. My pussy had been molded to his cock, but my body could never acclimate to his size quickly enough. He always felt enormous, always stretched me wide apart.

"Because I like it like this." He folded me underneath him, bringing our bodies as close together as possible. Then he started to rock, his forehead pressed to mine. He breathed with his thrusts, shook me with his movements. His arms flexed as he held his massive size on top of me.

My fingers ran through the back of his hair, feeling the short strands as I panted with his movements. Every time his cock was completely inside me, my knees shook just a little. He made me feel so full, like I couldn't accommodate even another centimeter. "You like to make love to me?"

His thrusts didn't stop, and he kept moving deep and slow. His breathing became rapid, and he pulled his forehead away from mine so he could look into my eyes. His eyes were locked on to my face, watching every reaction I made. He wore the concentrated expression that I adored, his face tinted with focus and desire. He wasn't thinking about anything else in the world but me. "I love it, Muse."

I READ THE NEWSPAPER WHILE THE TV WAS PLAYING IN the background. The coffee was freshly brewed, and my breakfast of bacon and eggs was warm. Room service was exactly the same thing that I got at home from Dante, but honestly, Dante's cooking was better.

His phone started to ring on the table.

I knew I shouldn't look, but I did.

Mama.

I was tempted to answer it, but I knew that would be wrong. It was his personal business, and I shouldn't cross the line. After last night, I felt more connected to him than I ever had before, but that still didn't mean I could do whatever I wanted.

I grabbed the phone and walked into the bathroom. The shower was on, and his naked body stood underneath the water. He ran his hands through his hair as he massaged the shampoo out of his strands.

It was a beautiful sight. "Conway, your mother is calling you. Do you want me to let it go to voice mail?"

"Answer it," he said as he tilted his head back under the stream. "I'm sure she would rather talk to you anyway."

I stepped back into the sitting room and took the call. "Hi, Pearl. It's Sapphire."

"Oh, hello," she said happily. "How's it going?"

"Conway is in the shower right now, so he told me to take your call." It might be weird to know we were in the same room together, and obviously, we were sleeping together and sharing our lives together. But his mother never made it weird.

"That's fine. I just wanted to congratulate him on last night. From all the headlines I've read, it seems like he blew them out of the water."

"He did. He got a standing ovation. I've never heard an

auditorium become so loud before." Not that I'd been in a lot of auditoriums.

"Yeah, I saw a few videos on TV. And there's an article circulating I think you'll find interesting."

"Yeah?"

"There're a few photos of you together. One where you two are pressing your foreheads together in the auditorium... It's sweet. There're a few others that catch Conway staring at you, wearing this look on his face..."

Redness immediately flowed into my cheeks, and I felt my neck light on fire. I wasn't just embarrassed but moved.

"My son is over the moon madly in love with you," she said with a sigh. "You have no idea how happy that makes me. All a mother wants is for her son to meet a woman who loves him as much as she does...just in a different way."

The crimson didn't die away. I listened to her words with sweaty palms, feeling ecstatic but unwell. Conway might be affectionate with me, but he'd never told me he loved me. Those three beautiful words had never come out of his mouth. But I didn't tell his mother that because it would just be too weird. I should just let her believe whatever she wanted.

"And I can tell you love him too."

Conway's laptop was sitting at the desk, so I helped myself to his computer and typed his name into Google.

Immediately, several articles surfaced about the show last night. One headline caught my attention, so I opened it.

Conway Barsetti Falls for His #1 Model.

When I clicked on it, several photos appeared. They were all from the show last night, capturing details between us that were candid and real. There was a picture of us kissing and another one of Conway staring at me when I came out of the bathroom. He ignored the reporter standing in front of him, his eyes trained on me with undeniable intensity.

I forgot his mother was on the phone because my heart was beating so fast.

Pearl spoke again. "Conway can call me back if he wants. But that's all I wanted to say. Do you know when you guys will be returning?"

"Uh." My mind was working furiously to do two things at once. I was staring at the pictures but also trying to focus on what she said. "No, I'm not sure. I think we're leaving tomorrow."

"That's great. We'll come for dinner so you guys can talk about your trip."

"That sounds good."

"Alright, I'll let you go," she said. "Talk to you later."

"Bye, Pearl."

"Bye."

I hung up and set his phone down. The second it touched the table, a message lit up on the screen.

It was from Vanessa. *You killed it last night, brother. So proud of you.* There were three heart emojis behind her words.

My eyes softened, loving the way Vanessa was affectionate with her brother. They bickered and argued a lot, but it was obvious they were loyal to each other.

I turned back to the screen and stared at the photographs of us together. My heart was beating so fast it actually hurt my chest. His mother believed we were in love, and when I stared at these pictures, it was difficult to believe otherwise.

We did look happy together.

I'd been so focused on my conversation with Pearl and the article that I hadn't noticed the shower was off. His footsteps sounded, and his voice emerged before he came around the corner. "What did my mother want?"

Frantically, I closed out of the article and put the laptop back where I found it. I jumped back into the seat and almost knocked over my cup of coffee. I caught it just as he rounded the corner, a towel around his waist.

He watched me with narrowed eyes. "Didn't mean to frighten you."

"You didn't." I cleared my throat and tried to act

natural. "I dropped my fork and knocked over my mug when I tried to pick it up...really stupid."

He kept staring at me, his gaze hard. But since that was the expression he usually wore, it was difficult to tell what he was thinking. He turned his gaze to his laptop and stared at it for several heartbeats.

Shit.

Then he moved to the seat across from me like nothing happened.

Fuck, did I not put it back exactly how it was? I hadn't been paying attention when I grabbed it.

He picked up the newspaper then poured the coffee into his mug.

Nothing seemed off.

But my heart was still pounding.

He drank his coffee then stared at me hard, his eyes narrowed. "Well?"

I grabbed my mug but didn't take a drink. My fingers wrapped around it, squeezing it hard enough that it could shatter. I forced myself to relax, to stop acting so guilty. I'd used his computer to look up something. That didn't make me evil. I guess I was just scared of what I saw. What would he think if he saw it? Would it annoy him? "Well...what?"

He took a long drink of his coffee as he stared at me. "What did my mother say?"

"Ohh..." I finally set down the mug and took a deep breath in relief.

He cocked an eyebrow. "And what did she say?" he pressed.

"She just wanted to congratulate you on your show last night. She said it was a hit, and she's very proud of you." I placed his cell phone in front of him, so he could see Vanessa's message. "She said you can call her back if you want, but you don't need to." I omitted all the other stuff she said, about him being madly in love with me.

Like the conversation never happened at all, he turned his gaze to the paper and ate quietly. He was still in just his towel, his damp hair slowly drying from the sunlight that filtered through the window. The hard lines of his body were more dramatic because the sun was causing shadows on his chiseled physique.

Last night, he made love to me before bed. He kissed me, took me gently, and stared into my eyes like he never wanted to stop. And now, he enjoyed the comfortable silence between us while reading his newspaper.

We seemed like a couple.

A man and a woman.

Maybe his mother was right. A picture was worth a thousand words.

And our pictures all said the same thousand words.

7
CONWAY

I WENT INTO THE OFFICE AND SAT BEHIND THE DESK while I spoke to Nicole. Muse was in the shower, and as much as she entertained me, I had to focus on my job. She distracted me so easily, but I had to be strong and stop that from happening so much.

"Enormous spike in sales, Conway. Just like last time, everything has sold out. Preorders are backing up, which brings me to the first issue at hand."

"I hate that word."

"Well, I'm not going to stop using it."

"What's the problem?"

"Your one distributor can't reach demand anymore. We need to take on a second."

Androssi. Dammit. I told him off, but now I might need him.

"I can take care of this for you, but I thought I would check with you first."

I'd let my pride cloud my judgment when I met with Androssi. I didn't appreciate anyone doubting my talents, not when I'd proven myself a million times over. But I shouldn't be so stubborn and let my temper cloud my thinking. "Get in touch with Androssi Beaucount. I'm sure he'd like the business."

Nicole picked up on my tone because she listened to it all the time. "Your meeting didn't go well?"

"A bit rocky. But I'm sure he'll be happy to do business now."

"He'd be stupid not to, regardless of his personal feelings for you."

I opened my laptop so I could access the documents she sent me.

"People were very thrilled to see Sapphire, even if she wasn't on stage. I think having her as your girlfriend was even better."

Girlfriend. I kept hearing that word over and over. "Yes, she was gorgeous." Once the screen turned on, I spotted my name typed into the Google search engine in the top right corner. I never looked myself up on the Internet, so I knew I hadn't typed it in there.

And only one person had access to my laptop.

Muse.

Why was she Googling me on my computer? I noticed she'd been jumpy when I walked into the room. And my laptop was placed in a way I hadn't left it. I just assumed I was being paranoid.

No, I wasn't paranoid at all.

"I just sent everything over," Nicole said. "Let me know when you're ready to go over them."

I opened a new tab and entered my name into the search engine. "Hold on, Nicole." A new page opened up with a list of headlines that all pertained to me, mainly my evening last night. The headlines were flattering, but there was one that was highlighted in a different color than all the rest.

The one that Muse clicked on.

I opened it and scanned the page. Someone had captured pictures of us together, of me kissing her and pressing my forehead to hers. They caught me staring at her. And there was an entire article written about me falling in love with my favorite model.

I wasn't sure how it made me feel.

A part of me wanted to scoff because it was ridiculous.

Another part of me felt a little terrified. The article was an opinion based on these pictures, but the photos themselves couldn't lie. I stared at her in a way I never stared at anyone else.

I was obviously obsessed with her.

How could I not be? She was beautiful in every picture, and she looked even more beautiful on my arm.

But I didn't love her. She didn't love me.

What these photographers captured was the intimacy between us, the friendship as well as the lust. Just because I didn't love her didn't mean I didn't care about her—and I cared about her so damn much. There was nothing I wouldn't do for her, nothing I wouldn't sacrifice for her. The world misinterpreted what they saw, what they thought they understood.

They knew nothing about us.

I closed the tab and went to my email. "I'm ready, Nicole."

WE RETURNED TO MILAN IN THE MIDDLE OF THE afternoon, and my men drove us back to Verona where my villa was waiting for me. Dante would have a full meal prepared, even though neither of us was hungry.

Muse looked out the window as she watched the countryside pass. She hadn't worn makeup during the flight, and now the sun blanketed her exquisite complexion with the perfect lighting. She was in jeans and a t-shirt, laid-back after the long journey.

I never told her I knew she used my computer. And I

never told her I knew what she was looking up.

I wondered what she thought about it.

Did she think I loved her?

I hoped not.

I never would.

We arrived at the house, and the men took our bags inside. The house was exactly the way we left it, clean, open, and bright. It was nice to be home. No amount of luxury at a five-star hotel could replace the comfort of my own place.

Our bags were set in the bedroom, and Muse immediately changed into a comfortable sundress.

It was still warm, but in the next few weeks, the weather would change drastically. It would get cold, start to rain, and soon after that, the snow would begin falling. The horses would be put in the stables, and I would be working from home almost exclusively to avoid the dangerous country roads.

"It's nice to be home." She hopped on the bed, bouncing up and down slightly as the mattress moved.

"It is."

"Your mother said she would love to get together for dinner and talk about our trip."

Now that the show was over, I had a little more time on my hands. Perhaps Muse and I would take a trip somewhere.

My phone rang, and Carter's name appeared on the screen. "Excuse me." I walked into the sitting room and sat on the couch before I took the call. I wasn't that far away, and she could probably still hear me, but anytime Muse was on my bed, I couldn't exactly think straight. "What's up, Carter?"

"Don't talk all casual like shit didn't just go down."

I stared out the window across my property. Horses were in the distance, and the flat countryside was breathtaking as it stretched on and on. "What shit went down, Carter? Are you referring to my show? Yes, it went well. Nicole told me sales are double what they were last time…"

"No, not that, asshole."

"Then what?" I asked with a sigh.

"All I see all over the news is that you're in love with this prisoner of yours. It's written all over your face, man."

Now he and the rest of the world had the same opinion. "I'm just being affectionate." I didn't say anything more because I didn't want Muse to overhear me. "Is there something else you wanted to talk about?"

"I just don't understand why you don't admit it. You've never been the kind of guy to pretend to be something you aren't."

"And I'm not pretending now," I said calmly. "If you have nothing else to say, I'm hanging up."

"She's there, isn't she?" he asked. "Gotcha."

"Yes," I said in confirmation.

"Alright," he said. "I guess we'll talk about it later."

"No, we won't be talking about this later. We won't be talking about this ever."

"Whatever," Carter scoffed. "I've got another call. It's for Yasmine something… She's from Israel."

These calls were good because they made me rich. But they were also bad because it reminded me of how this world really was. Evil men lurked around every corner. There was no amount of opposition that could fight it. "When?"

"Tonight. You can make it, right?"

Did I have much of a choice? "Yes."

"Alright. I'll send you a picture. Her parents are pretty shaken up."

"As they should be." If any woman I cared about were in that position, I wouldn't be able to sleep. "How much?"

"Fifteen million."

That was seven and a half for each of us. I only had to do this ten times to make back the money I shelled out for Muse. I was digging myself out of a very expensive hole. "Alright."

"Let me know how it goes."

"Hold on. I'm dropping Yasmine off at your place."

"My place?" he asked incredulously. "That's not how

this works. I took one of the girls just because of the situation—"

"Muse lives with me now. And I don't want another woman in the house. One is enough."

"But Muse isn't just some woman. She's your—"

"I'm risking my neck by showing up there with no guns and no backup. This is the least you can do, Carter."

He sighed into the phone. "Fine."

"Bye." I hung up and tossed the phone onto the coffee table. I stared out the window, suddenly craving a cigar. I'd love to pull the smoke into my lungs and let my body absorb the nicotine. I wasn't some pussy who did whatever Muse asked, but I knew she would pluck it out of my mouth the second she saw me with it.

I couldn't even enjoy it.

Muse came up behind me and glided her hands down my chest. She leaned over me and sprinkled my neck with kisses.

I closed my eyes and treasured the feeling of her soft lips, of the way they felt against my warm skin. Her breath washed over me, erotic and wonderful. My hand moved on top of hers, and I craned my neck harder, wanting Muse to take as much as she wanted.

This was much better than the cigar anyway.

She straightened behind me and pulled her hands away. "Are you going somewhere tonight?"

So, she could hear. "Yes."

Her hands moved to my shoulders and massaged my muscles. "Am I coming along?"

She obviously had no idea where I was going if she asked that question. "No. I'm going to the Underground."

Her hands stopped. "Are you buying someone?"

"Yes."

"I see..." She started to massage me again. "Who is it this time?"

"A woman from Israel. I don't know much about her right now."

"Is she staying here?"

"No. She'll stay with Carter."

"Poor thing. She must be terrified."

They were all terrified.

"Does your father know you do this?"

He didn't have a clue. No one in the family did. My father would scold me for getting mixed up with the Skull Kings, and my mother would hate me if she knew I was saving women for cash. Uncle Cane wouldn't like it either. "No."

"How long as this been going on?"

"For about five years. Ever since my father told me about my aunt Vanessa."

"I admire what you're doing, but I think it's too dangerous..." She walked around the couch and took a seat beside me on the cushion. "The men there are evil, Conway."

Everyone was evil. "It'll be fine."

She still wore the same look of terror. "Can I wait in the car?"

"Absolutely not." I didn't want her anywhere nearby.

"Can I wait at your apartment?"

"No."

"Conway—"

"You're staying here. End of story."

She shut her mouth, but her eyes showed her disappointment.

"If you think I'd ever let you anywhere near a place like that again, you're out of your mind." Now the comfort of her kisses had evaporated, and I couldn't feel her lips on my skin anymore. I grabbed the pack of cigars on the table.

She snatched them out of my hand. "Conway."

I stared at her incredulously, unable to believe the stunt she just pulled. "Muse, don't test me."

"Don't test *me*," she replied. "You don't want me to go with you to the Underground, fine. But enough with these." She held them up in my face. "As long as I'm living in this house, they're forbidden."

"This is my house, in case you've forgotten."

"And I'm the woman of this house." She pulled the cigars out of the box and shoved them into a glass full of water, ruining them instantly. "No cigars." She strutted off, shaking her hips with attitude as she went.

I stared at her ass as she stormed off to the bedroom, loving the way it shook with all that sass. When she was gone, I faced forward again and stared at the ruined cigars that I smoked with Carter every time I was with him. If she really wanted something, she fought for it. Like the cigars, for instance. But the things she was most passionate about concerned my well-being. She cared more about keeping me healthy than anything else, even if that meant pissing me off.

For reasons I couldn't understand, that got me hard.

I TOOK THE SECRET ENTRANCE TO THE BASEMENT OF the opera house and was checked at the entryway. They patted me down, searching for guns and knives. When they didn't find anything, they allowed me passage inside.

Moving across the red carpet, I entered the dark room where the gentlemen sat. A topless woman was walking around taking drink orders, her massive tits earning her a fortune in tips.

I took a seat in my usual spot and didn't stare at the men around me.

Because it was a rule.

No eye contact. No gawking. No identifying.

What happened at the Underground stayed at the Underground. If I saw a famous politician or a celebrity, it was forbidden to report it. If I did, it would result in permanent expulsion from the Underground as well as a hefty fine.

Big Tits came over with my drink on a tray. "Scotch on the rocks, right?"

I didn't look at her. "Yes."

"And two cigars." She set them on the table.

I didn't gawk at her tits anyway, but now I felt uncomfortable even looking at them. Staring wasn't cheating, but it somehow felt disrespectful to Muse. Why would I look at this woman's tits when I had a perfect woman waiting for me at home? She cared about me, respected me. She would never step foot inside this place again, so she would never know what I was looking at it.

But she made me want to be honorable…for whatever reason.

"I don't need the cigars." I drank the scotch.

"Alright." She placed them in her apron then serviced the other men.

Smoke filled the room and got into my lungs, but as tempting as it was, I shook it off.

Another man walked inside and sat at the table beside me. He was in my line of sight, so I noticed the black leather jacket he wore along with the rest of his black clothing. The sleeves of his jacket were pushed up, showing the black ink on his skin. His jaw hadn't been shaved in days, so he had a heavy shadow across his features. With dark eyes and dark hair, he looked like a classic Italian.

I had no idea who he was.

The women were brought on stage, tied up and buck naked. And then the bidding started.

I stared at them because that's what I was expected to do. Shaking and afraid, they didn't look desirable at all. They reminded me of innocent sheep about to be slaughtered. People assumed they were too stupid to know what was going on, but they could sense it. They would be treated with malice and cruelty before they were finally drowned or shot between the eyes. Unfortunately, death was the best part.

Yasmine was in the middle. She was a slender girl with beautiful eyes. She looked way too young to be up there. She definitely wasn't eighteen yet, and that made this situation even more disgusting. The men would pay a lot of money for her.

The bidding started.

One of the women in the beginning was particularly beautiful, so that bidding lasted longer than usual. But eventually, some asshole won her and wore a cruel sneer in victory. They moved farther down the row, selling each woman because the captors were no longer human.

The only man besides me who didn't bid on anyone was the young guy close by. He sat with his ankles crossed and his hand wrapped around his beer. He didn't even grab his paddle in preparation to buy someone.

I hoped he wasn't after Yasmine.

Most of the men in the Underground were much older, in their forties, fifties, and even sixties. They were grotesque, which was why they had to buy a woman rather than pick one up on their own.

But this guy in the leather jacket was different.

He was young, good-looking, and obviously wealthy.

Who the hell was he?

We finally arrived at Yasmine.

I raised my paddle. "Five hundred thousand." I started off low so I wouldn't be suspicious.

She reached two million immediately. Then it jumped to four, seven, and then ten.

"Fifteen million." I lowered my paddle. I just spent a hundred million on Muse a few months ago, so no one would raise an eyebrow to my bid.

No one challenged it.

"Sold to Mr. Barsetti." There was one more girl on the stage, so the bidding started over.

Leather Jacket didn't bid on her either.

If he wasn't there to pick up a woman, what was he doing?

Was he spying? Was he with the feds? I found that unlikely. No way he would have made it past the background check if he was dirty.

The last girl was sold off, and then the Skull King at the front stared at Leather Jacket. "None of the women up here good enough for you, Bones?"

My blood had never turned so ice-cold in my life.

My heart even stopped beating in my chest, and that never happened, not even for Muse.

I was sick to my stomach and pissed off all at the same time.

Bones? Did I hear that right?

My father told me the Barsettis had a blood war with Bones, an arms dealer who sold illegal weaponry. My father never explained the details and never explained how my grandparents died. But he did mention the name of the man who killed my aunt, the man my father had killed before I was born.

His name was Bones.

But this guy was my age, maybe a little older.

Was it just a coincidence?

Could a name like that be a coincidence in circles like these?

The man drank his beer before wiping his mouth with

the back of his forearm. The corner of his mouth rose in a lazy grin, and he filled the room with such confidence that it was borderline cocky.

Cockier than me.

He finally answered. "Nah. I'm not good enough for them."

Yasmine sobbed as I dragged her out of the Underground to my SUV, which was parked at the curb. She was dressed in the sweatpants and t-shirt I brought along. It was difficult to escort a naked woman to my car in public, even under the cover of darkness. The police looked the other way, but we didn't parade it around so visibly.

I got into the car and drove away.

Tears rolled down her cheeks, and she cried so hard she could barely breathe.

Most annoying fucking sound in the world.

Muse didn't cry. She held her ground and didn't back down. She didn't accept defeat, even when she had no other option. I respected her for it.

I didn't respect this. "Calm down, Yasmine. It'll be alright."

She cried harder.

God, the noise was hurting my ears.

I pulled a knife from my pocket and then slit the rope between her wrists. "Look, I'm not going to hurt you. I'm not going to touch you. You're okay."

She rubbed the chafed skin of her wrists and stared at me hesitantly, finally no longer crying.

She should jump out of the car or attack me.

I was disappointed when she didn't. Women should be taught to fight, fight to the death. That's what my father had taught Vanessa since she was a teenager. "Your parents paid me to get you out of there. I'm dropping you off at my cousin's house, and you're staying there for a while. When it's no longer suspicious, we'll send you back to Israel." I was grateful my tech team had been able to install new security measures on my car, so I could once again talk freely while driving.

"But you just spent so much money on me…"

"Not me. Your parents."

"Oh, thank god." She covered her face with her hands and took a deep breath. "Thank you… Thank you. I've never been so scared—"

"Don't thank me. Your parents paid handsomely for your return." I didn't care about consoling her, not when I had other things on my mind. Right now, all I could think about was the man who called himself Bones. He was an arrogant son of a bitch. I didn't like him. Something in my gut told me he was foul.

I parked in the roundabout at Carter's place and walked her inside.

"You don't knock anymore?" Carter walked into the entryway in just his sweatpants. Fit like me, he had the same Barsetti build that made women want to fuck us all the time.

Yasmine immediately looked away, like the sight of his bare chest was forbidden.

"Pull on a shirt, asshole." I walked with Yasmine into the living room. "She's sixteen."

"Knock, asshole." Carter pulled on the t-shirt sitting across the back of the couch. "Then I would have been dressed."

"You knew I was coming."

"Whatever." He ran his fingers through his partially damp hair, evidently having just gotten out of the shower. "How'd it go?"

"The process wasn't out of the ordinary." I turned to Yasmine. "You're probably starving, right?"

She nodded.

"Carter, you got food for her?" I asked.

"Yeah." Carter nodded to the kitchen. "There's a sandwich in the fridge, but you can have whatever you want."

Yasmine slowly walked away, heading into the kitchen. Once she was out of earshot, I faced him again.

"Something did happen," I said. "And you aren't going to believe it."

He crossed his arms over his chest. "Try me."

"There was this young guy there tonight. Never seen him before in my life. Good-looking, arrogant—"

"Stop scoping out the dudes and get to the point."

I narrowed my eyes. "I noticed he didn't fit. And he didn't bid on a single woman."

Carter finally tensed, his suspicion rising. "Not once?"

"No. And there was plenty of talent tonight. But then the Skull King doing the auction spoke to him. His name was Bones."

Just as I did when I first heard the name, Carter turned pale. His skin became creamy white like milk. Even his lips changed color. His eyes dilated like a light had been shined right in his eyes. His arms lowered to his sides and he released a deep breath. "Are you sure?"

"Un-fucking-mistakable."

"Did he know who you were?"

"The Skull King said my name, but he didn't react to it."

"Bones...that's just not right. How can that be his name?"

"I don't get it either."

"Any relation?" Carter asked.

I shook my head. "My father told me he didn't have any children."

"Unless he didn't know about them. Maybe he had a mistress who was pregnant. Bones Sr. died, so she named him after his father."

"I guess it's possible…"

"Or he could just be a lunatic wanting to be like Bones."

"That's possible too," I said quietly.

"Or maybe it's a coincidence. He just likes the name."

I shook my head. "Unlikely. When you run in those circles, there are no coincidences."

Carter stepped back and rubbed his hand across his jaw. "Fuck…"

"Should we talk to our fathers about it?"

"Are you kidding me?" he asked. "How would we explain how we know about it in the first place?"

"The truth."

He shook his head. "They'd break our faces."

"Probably." It's not like we didn't deserve it. My father would be disappointed in me if he knew about any of this.

"So, the guy didn't even look at you?" he asked incredulously. "Barsetti meant nothing to him?"

"It seemed that way."

"But if he didn't buy a woman, maybe he was just

there to spy on you."

"How would he have known I was coming? I didn't even know I was going until this afternoon."

"Unless he goes to every meeting in the hope of running into you."

My blood turned ice-cold again.

"I don't trust that name, Conway. Anyone with a name like that...is an enemy to all Barsettis."

"I know." The guy didn't give his name willingly. The Skull King was the one who put him on the spot. He didn't seem threatening, but every man in that room was wealthy and violent. If we were locked in a room together during a war, none of us would get out alive. "The next step is telling our fathers."

"I don't know...let's think about it."

"I think they have a right to know. They think Bones had no one to avenge him."

"And he's had nearly thirty years to avenge his father, but he hasn't."

"Well, he probably wasn't old enough until now."

"And we're assuming they're related when we have no idea," Carter replied. "I don't want to bother them until there's a legitimate reason to bother them. And I'm not giving us up without a good reason. Otherwise, we're just going to piss our fathers off for no reason."

"Then what do we do?" I asked. "Are you going to look

into this?"

"Yeah, I'll ask around," Carter said. "But I'll be hush-hush about it. Don't want to draw attention to myself and provoke him needlessly."

"True." I shoved my hands into my pockets, and despite the crazy night I'd had, I was anxious to get home to Muse. I wanted to tell her about my night, make love with her tits in my face, then go to sleep. "Let me know what you find out."

"I will."

I was about to walk out when my phone vibrated with a text message. I pulled it out of my pocket and saw Muse's name on the screen. *I'm sorry to bother you, but it's four and you still aren't back...tell me you're alright.*

She wasn't checking up on me because she was worried I was messing around behind her back. She just wanted to know I was alright, that I hadn't been caught by the Skull Kings. If this were months ago, I would have been ticked by the question. But I knew Muse truly cared about me.

Carter glanced at my phone and grinned. "Get home to your wife."

I didn't bother with a rebuttal. I just walked out and got into the car. The house was right down the road so I would be home in less than five minutes, but I texted her back anyway. *I'll be home in five minutes.*

Thank you.

I WALKED INTO THE BEDROOM AND FOUND HER SITTING up in bed. She was ready for sleep, dressed in one of my t-shirts with her makeup removed from her face. Her long brown hair was pulled over one shoulder. Despite her obvious exhaustion, she was alert the second I walked in the door. "I'm so glad you're back."

I pulled my tie through my collar and dropped my suit jacket on the ground. I walked to the bed and leaned down to kiss her on the mouth. I gave her a quick kiss, the kind a husband gave his wife when he came home from work. "I'm surprised you're still awake." Clothes dropped on the floor, and I stripped until I was in my boxers.

"Couldn't sleep..."

I pulled back the covers and got into bed beside her. "Jet lag?"

"No." She immediately cuddled into my side like she hadn't seen me in days rather than hours. "I just can't sleep unless you're next to me." She spoke into my chest, her soft hair grazing over my arm.

I stared down at her face, catching the sincerity in her eyes. I'd been anxious to get home, but knowing she was waiting for me only made me more eager. I was a man of solitude and didn't like answering to anyone, but I enjoyed having someone to come home to. "I'm here now."

"I know." She breathed a happy sigh. "And now I'm so happy…"

I turned off the bedside lamp, plunging the bedroom into darkness. I let it surround us and listened to her gentle breathing. I had so much to tell her, but now I enjoyed our quiet companionship.

Her arm trailed down my chest, her fingertips lightly touching me. "Did it go well?"

"Yes. I dropped Yasmine off at Carter's. She's very young. I'm glad she'll be going home."

"Me too," she said.

I debated telling her about Bones, but she was so peaceful that I didn't want to upset her. I'd never cared about protecting someone, but now I wanted to surround her in a bubble of fantasy. I didn't want her to know about the horrific shit waiting just outside my gates because I wanted her to be happy. I wanted her to feel safe by my side, to know that nothing outside these walls could hurt her—not with me around.

So, I kept it to myself.

My fingers moved under her chin, and I directed her gaze up to me. "Make love to me, Muse."

Her lips parted slightly, showing her small teeth behind her plump lips. A quiet breath escaped her mouth, moving over my skin and warming my lips. She turned her face to my chest and pressed kisses everywhere, kissing my hard muscles and searing skin. Then she climbed on top of me and straddled my hips.

"Show me how much you missed me."

She yanked down my boxers until my cock was free, and she pulled her thong to the side so I could slide inside. She pressed my crown to her entrance then slowly slid all the way down. Biting her bottom lip as she moved, she took in my big dick slowly. Once she had all of it, she sat on my lap for a few seconds to get used to it.

My hands moved to her hips. "No shirt."

She pulled it over her head, revealing her perfect tits.

"Yes..." My palms gripped her perky bosom, feeling her hard nipples and soft skin. I played with them, massaging them greedily. Everything about her was perfect, from her rack to the curve of her bottom lip.

She started to move, slowly sheathing my dick and pulling out again. She moved precisely, breathing heavily every time she took my length deep inside her. Her breath was husky, full of desire.

My hands guided her hips, showing her how to rub her clit just right.

She breathed louder and deeper, her hands gripping my shoulders for balance. "I missed you..."

"Yeah?" My hand dug into her hair and pulled it back

from her face. "How much?"

"So much." She pressed her forehead against mine.

"Can't sleep without me?"

"No..." She bit her bottom lip and kept moving. She took my dick so well, her tight cunt perfect for my big cock.

"Why?"

"I...I don't know."

I started to rock back into her, beginning to push my cock back inside her. "Yes, you do. Tell me."

"I just... You make me feel safe."

My cock twitched inside her, loving that answer. "Because you're always safe with me."

Her nails started to claw into my skin. She ground her clit against my pelvic bone, her body slowly writhing because of the way it made her feel. She succumbed to her desire, fell prey to the way I made her pussy tighten.

"And you need my come, don't you?" My lips devoured her neck, lavishing her with full kisses and the gentle bites from my teeth. I rolled her hips as we moved together, both of our bodies writhing as one.

"Yes..." She held on to me and pressed her forehead to mine as she came, squeezing my dick so hard it would leave a bruise. Sweat trickled down her neck to her gorgeous tits, and her eyes turned lidded and heavy as euphoria washed over her. She came with endless moans, filling my bedroom with her hypnotic voice and making infinite echoes.

I watched her little performance, watched the way her eyes locked on to mine as she enjoyed every second of her high. My fat dick was doing its job by pleasing her. I never got so much satisfaction as watching a woman come. Watching her feel good made me feel good. I'd please her all night without getting any satisfaction of my own because just being inside her was enough for me.

She dug her nails into my shoulders and kept rocking. "Give it to me, Conway."

I squeezed her waist so hard I thought I might crush her. My thumbs pressed into her rib cage, and I felt my dick twitch inside her.

"You want my come, Muse?"

"Please..." She ground into me harder, her gorgeous tits shaking in my face.

My jaw tightened, and my balls pulled closer to my body. I felt the climax approach over the horizon, felt it rush through all my veins and nerves. My cock seared with heat, and I felt my crown explode. "Fuck..." I pulled her tight on my lap, letting my come fill her tight little cunt. I gave her every single drop, gave her all my arousal. My face pressed into her tits as I finished, my come mixing with hers.

So damn good.

I kissed the area between her tits and sucked her nipples, aroused by my satisfaction. I'd had a long night dealing with the underworld, but the second I came home, all of that shit was left at the door. All I cared about was making love, not thinking about my hatred.

She stayed on my lap, my cock softening inside her. Her hands ran up and down my chest, her fingertips now gentle to make up for the way she gripped me before. Now I was home, and she was satisfied, so she could roll over and go to sleep. But she stayed parked on my lap. "I want more."

My hands gripped her cheeks, and I squeezed them in my fingertips. "More what?"

She pressed her forehead to mine, her tits pressing against my chest. "You."

I WORKED IN MY OFFICE AND WENT OVER REPORTS WITH Nicole. Androssi was now on board for production, but he hadn't acquired all of my business. Now the work had been split between two different companies since I had so many orders to fill.

Fuck you, Androssi.

Preorders had spiked all over the globe, from Russia to Budapest.

I'd topped my best week by double.

I had lunch in my office and kept working, and once

two o' clock came around, I lost interest. I walked to the window and stared at the stables in the distance. I could see the horses, and when I looked at the stables, I could see Muse walking back and forth, carrying feed or hay.

When I looked at her, my recent accomplishments seemed insignificant.

Topping my previous sales week was only important because it reflected my quality. Money didn't matter as much as it used to—because I had so much of it. Now that Muse was an integral part of my life, I cared far more about my reputation than the size of my wallet.

Because Muse didn't seem to care about my money.

She was always impressed by the way people treated me, by the way my family loved me.

I stared at her through the window for a few minutes longer, watching her work in the humid weather as she busted her ass around the property. She had a difficult job, but not once did she complain.

She loved it.

My father respected her for working so hard.

I did too.

It would be easy for her to lie by the pool every day and go shopping for things she didn't need.

But she never cared about that.

She cared about me.

I walked down to the stables where she was working,

and I saw the jean shorts she wore up close. Short and dirty, they showed off her long, tanned legs and her boots. Her plaid shirt was tied around her waist, and she wore a white Stetson hat.

Damn, she looked fuckable.

I came up behind her, my eyes on her tight and perky ass. "Muse."

She turned around quickly, a bright smile on her face that wasn't there a moment ago. "What brings you down here?" She tilted her hat back slightly to reveal more of her face. Free of makeup with a little dirt on her cheek, she looked naturally perfect.

"You." She was the only reason I did anything anymore.

"Me?" She rose on her tiptoes and kissed me on the mouth. "That's a nice surprise. But I'm working right now. I've got to feed and groom the horses."

"You can't take a break for me?" I asked.

"Well, maybe a short one." Her hands moved over my forearms, feeling the veins underneath my skin. "What did you have in mind?"

"I actually wanted to see if you wanted to take a ride with me. There's a nice path down the street from my property. It goes through the hills, the oak trees, and to a nice spot where we can have dinner at sunset."

Now her work at the stables seemed insignificant

because she was so thrilled. "Really?"

"Yeah." I couldn't stop the smile from forming across my face. When she was happy, it was infectious. Like the common cold, I caught it.

"I'd love to."

"Alright. I'll have Dante pack us something to eat, and we'll leave in an hour."

"Can I take my own horse?"

"If you want," I said. "Or we could both take Carbine."

"Hmm...I could have my own horse, or I could have my arms wrapped around a gorgeous man the whole way. Let me think about that."

My smile deepened. "Gorgeous man, huh?"

"Hell yeah."

I chuckled. "Let me know what you decide."

I STRAPPED THE FOOD ONTO THE SIDE OF CARBINE'S saddle then pulled myself up. I sat close to the horn then extended my hand to Muse.

"You think he can carry both of us?"

I rolled my eyes. "You weigh nothing, Muse."

"But you weigh two hundred pounds."

"Carbine could carry ten of us. He'll be alright."

She finally took my hand and landed in the saddle

behind me. Her arms wrapped around my waist, and she rested her chin on my shoulder. "I'm excited."

I clicked my tongue and guided Carbine out the gate and onto the street. We walked along the road until we found the dirt path and began our journey. The fields were golden, and the breeze was a little cooler now that fall was approaching. She and I enjoyed our mutual silence as we took in the beautiful views. Once we reached the top of the hill, we could see all of Verona at the bottom.

"Wow," she said. "That's so beautiful."

Visiting New York City taught me to appreciate what I had. I had the clean air, wide open spaces, and silence. I was surrounded by natural beauty, by fields that had been claimed for thousands of years. The city of Verona was one of the oldest cities in Italy—and it was right outside my door.

We rode for another thirty minutes until we found the spot I was looking for. An oak tree stood tall on the crest of the hill, the large branches casting a perfect shadow to shield us from the heat. I stopped Carbine in place and helped Muse down before I made my way to the ground.

Muse walked around him in her jean shorts and t-shirt, her curled hair trailing behind her back. She stood under the tree and stared up at the filtering sunlight, looking like a flower on the hillside. Even when she did the most casual things, she looked absolutely stunning.

I watched her for a moment before I unpacked the blanket and set it across the ground. I grabbed the bag of food next, stuffed with a cold dinner and ice packs to keep the food preserved. I sat the bag on the blanket before taking a seat.

"Does Carbine need to be tied up?" she asked. "He's pretty ornery at the stables."

"He's fine." He was a moody horse, but he always obeyed me. He never trailed too far away, our minds connected in a special way between a man and his horse.

Muse sat beside me and pulled out the dinner Dante packed for her. Everything was placed in plastic cases, every part of the dinner organized into separate compartments. Fine silver forks were included, along with bottles of water. I didn't bring wine because that would be too complicated.

Muse stared at Verona, watching the sunlight shine across the beautiful architecture of the city. "When your mom and I were there, she took me to see Juliet's balcony."

I'd passed by it a few times but never cared enough to stop and look. "What did you think?"

"It was beautiful. It's hard to grasp the idea that something is that old... Everything in America is relatively new."

"I understand what you mean."

"And there were all these people leaving letters, even men. Have you seen *Letters to Juliet*?"

I stopped eating and stared at her blankly. "I'm not sure what that is."

"It's a movie, a romantic movie."

I turned back to my dinner. "Do I strike you as a man who watches romance movies?"

She elbowed me in the side playfully. "Don't be rude."

I nudged her back, but gently. "I'm not. I can't even remember the last movie I watched. I hardly watch TV, unless it's the news."

"Well, it's this movie that takes place in Verona. A woman discovers a letter that hasn't been answered by Juliet, so she answers it herself. There's more to it than that, but it's sweet. To see the place in person…was pretty incredible."

"I didn't realize you wanted to see it so much." A twinge of guilt burned in my chest, feeling stupid for not taking her there myself. The parts of Italy she'd seen involved her being homeless, so the experience couldn't have been that great. I could give her a whole different experience of Italy, if I weren't so focused on my next line that I needed to debut to the world.

"I didn't either until your mom mentioned it. I totally forgot it was in Verona. Such a romantic place."

"We're technically in Verona right now." I set my

plastic entrée container off to the side, finished with the meal Dante threw together. My arms rested on my knees as I stared at the city in front of us, watching the light change as it reflected off the rooftops of the ancient buildings.

She turned to me, a slight smile on her lips. "I know..." She turned back to her food and took a few more bites. "It surprises me that Dante can whip up something so good. It sat in the saddlebags for forty-five minutes and it's cold, but it's still great."

"He did train at the culinary institute in Milan."

"No surprise there..." She kept eating until the container was empty. Then she returned the lid to the top and set it aside.

Carbine grazed nearby, eating stalks of grass and staying within fifty feet of us. He was a well-trained horse, and he wouldn't ride off anywhere. He had an attitude and didn't respond to people he didn't know well, but once that bond was formed, he was extremely loyal.

She pulled her knees to her chest as she sat beside me, her curled hair catching the wind from time to time.

The sight in front of us was perfect, but I kept wanting to stare at her instead.

"So, what's next for Conway Barsetti?" she asked.

"What do you mean?" My elbow touched hers as we sat on the wool blanket. I was in jeans and a t-shirt, and it was one of the rare times I wore boots. Since I was inside all the time, I usually wore casual shoes.

"You just reached a new height for your career. Does that mean you'll get back to the studio right away?"

The sun started to set behind us, bringing the rooftops into brighter and more brilliant color. But as the sun continued on its trajectory, that brilliance started to fade. Light began to dissipate. "I don't think so. It's time for a break."

"Really?" she asked. "You don't strike me as the kind of man who takes breaks."

"I've had more success than most people in the world, and I'm not even thirty yet. My father told me to slow things down and take time to appreciate these great moments. Before we know it, time will pass and our youth will be gone."

"Very wise," she whispered. "Your father seems to know everything."

"Yes, he's always right…" Even when I didn't want him to be.

"So, what are you going to do? Sit around and watch TV? Take up a new hobby?"

"No," I answered. "I have only one hobby."

"Which is?"

"Travel. I'm thinking of taking a trip to Greece. I have a yacht and a villa in Santorini."

Her eyes lit up like fireworks, and her grin was adorable. "Uh...are you planning on taking anyone with you?" She pivoted her body and pressed her tits into my shoulder as her hand snaked down my arm. "Because, I don't have any plans..."

"Don't you have work in the stables?"

Her grin dropped. "Marco can handle it while I'm gone."

"I don't know..." I was going to milk this as much as I could. I loved her enthusiasm, the way she got so excited the second I mentioned the trip. Spending the afternoon on my yacht in the Mediterranean with this beautiful woman laying out in her bikini sounded like the perfect vacation to me. We'd make the boat rock together. "And what are you going to do for me while we're there?"

She pressed her face close to mine, her hands moving over the veins in my forearms. "Whatever you want..."

Good fucking answer.

She moved in closer and kissed the corner of my mouth, her lips dragging over the stubble on my chin. My coarse hair was rough, and I liked feeling her soft lips drag against it. "I know you don't need inspiration right now... but I can do other things."

"You have my attention."

She continued to massage my arm, her lips still treasuring my jawline. "I can please you every night. I can suck you off on your yacht, let you fuck me in the ass in the hull of your boat…whatever you want."

She was making a strong argument. "Alright. I'll take you."

She smiled against my mouth and squeezed my forearm. "Thank you. I've always wanted to go."

I lay back against the blanket and patted my chest, directing her to lie next to me.

She moved beside me, taking the same position she did when we were in bed together. My arm circled her waist while the other rested on her knee. My thumb brushed the soft skin of her knee, and the scent of her hair flooded me the second she was against me.

We couldn't see the city anymore, but the sky was a beautiful sight. Mixed with bright colors from the sunset, it was a wonder to behold. The stars slowly started to emerge, bright lights in the dark background of infinite space.

She trailed her fingers down my chest. "Thanks for bringing me here."

"I didn't bring you here. Carbine did."

"You know what I mean," she said with a chuckle. "It's beautiful… I love lying in the grass with the breeze in my hair. I didn't realize how much I loved being outdoors until I came here. Now, I couldn't imagine spending my life anywhere else."

Anywhere else in the world? Or anywhere else without me?

Why did I even care?

"You didn't miss New York when you were there?"

"Not really," she said. "I enjoyed my time living there, getting tacos in the middle of the night when I was studying, and riding the subway when I needed to get uptown. It's beautiful in its own way. But now that I've experienced something like this, I'm not sure if I could go back. I've had some bad experiences here, obviously. But the good far outweigh the bad."

"Do those experiences have anything to do with me?" I stared at the sky and watched the colors change slightly, shifting from splashes of orange and pink to blue and purple. The question came out of my mouth on its own. If my logic had been quicker, I never would have asked the question.

She sat up and raised her head over mine. She looked down into my face, her hair pulled over one shoulder. My fingers immediately migrated to the back of her head, feeling those soft strands with my fingertips. I supported her slightly, my eyes glued to tilt at the corner of her mouth. Her hand slid up my chest until she cupped my face. Then she leaned in and pressed her mouth to mine, giving me a soft kiss that was as gentle as a rose petal. But the softness didn't cushion the passion behind it. Her deep intake of breath showed her emotion, and her fingers cupped my face harder as the embrace continued. "Yes... they have everything to do with you."

My bags were packed and ready to be hauled to the car. Muse didn't need as much time to get her stuff together because I had Dante buy her everything she needed. She had a lot of clothes in my closet, but none that were appropriate for a Greek getaway to the Mediterranean.

Carter's name popped up on the screen when he called.

I stepped out of the bedroom so that the men could collect our things and put them in the trunk. I walked into Muse's old bedroom, the place where she used to sleep alone every night. That seemed like a lifetime ago now. It was hard to imagine her anywhere else but right on my chest.

I took the call. "What did you find?"

Carter didn't make small talk and jumped right into the conversation. "Nothing. I've discreetly asked about him through my various channels, but no one is talking. And the fact that no one is talking is what concerns me."

"Because they don't have an allegiance to you?"

"It's not about loyalty. This is about fear. They obviously fear this guy."

That was disconcerting. "There's gotta be a way to dig up information on him. Someone knows something."

"Yeah...but I don't want to arouse suspicion by asking too many questions. Sometimes when a man tries to avoid his destiny, he only brings himself to it quicker."

"Been eating Chinese food?" I asked.

"What?" he asked blankly.

"You sound like a damn fortune cookie."

"Shut up, Con," he snapped. "This is serious shit."

"And when shit is serious, that's the time to make a joke."

He released a sigh into the phone. "I'm not sure what to do. You got any ideas?"

I knew a few people in the Underground ring. But I wasn't sure if any of them knew anything. "There's one person who definitely knows."

"Who?"

"Iron, the Skull King that ran the bid the other night. Pointed him out by name."

"True."

"Maybe I could ask him."

"But that's also dangerous," Carter said. "If you ask him, he'll probably tell Bones you're asking questions."

Fuck. "You're right."

"You need to have someone else ask. Make it less suspicious."

"Like who?" I sat on the bed and listened to the men carry everything down the hallway. Muse's light footsteps followed behind them as she headed down the stairway and to entryway on the first floor.

Carter considered it in silence. Minutes passed, and he didn't say anything. "I have an idea, but you aren't going to like it."

"Then maybe I shouldn't bother listening to it."

He ignored me. "Sapphire. If a beautiful woman asks questions, they might not think anything of it."

My hand immediately tightened into a fist at the question. "You're right. This idea is idiotic, and I don't want to bother talking about it anymore."

"Then we can find someone else. But if we have a woman ask, it might make it less suspicious."

"Like who?"

"I don't know…is there a waitress there?"

Yes, there was. Cynthia. At least that's what she said her name was. "Yeah."

"Pay her off."

"Still risky. She might tell the Skull Kings what I'm doing."

"Not if you pay her enough. Ten grand oughta do it."

"Maybe. But her fear of death could be stronger than

cash." The Skull Kings operated in broad daylight because no one was stupid enough to fuck with them. They were untouchable. "I say we get a different woman."

"Like a whore?"

"Skull Kings don't fuck whores."

"Then Cynthia is our only choice."

She was the only person who could get away with the questions. She served the men in the Underground, so she could just ask Bones these questions herself. "When I get back, I'll talk to her."

"Get back from where?" he asked.

"Sapphire and I are taking a trip to Greece."

"Are you fucking kidding me? At a time like this?"

"I finished my show, and now I want a vacation."

"But, right now?" he spat. "We need to get this going."

I looked at my watch, noticing the time. It was almost eight in the evening. I was taking my private plane to Santorini, so I could put it off as long as I wanted. "I'll handle Cynthia tonight before I leave. Then I'll have her call me when she knows more."

"Alright, that works. There's an auction tonight, ironically."

"Then I'll go."

"Just bid on a woman and don't buy one. That shouldn't be suspicious."

"Yeah."

"Okay, let me know how it goes." He hung up.

I put my phone back into my pocket and walked to the entryway. Muse was waiting, wearing a long blue dress with a pink cardigan. She was already dressed for Greece, even though we wouldn't be there for a while.

"Everything alright?" she asked.

With the men hanging around, I couldn't answer her. "Yeah. We just need to make a stop on the way."

I parked in the underground garage, and we took the elevator to my place on the top floor of the building.

Muse stood beside me, her purse over her arm. "What are we doing here?"

"I just need to take care of something really quick." The doors opened directly into my living room.

Muse stepped inside and sat on one of the plush couches. She didn't turn on the TV or grab one of the magazines on the table. Judging by the way she didn't get comfortable, she assumed I just needed to grab something.

"I need you to stay here for a little bit. I'll be back in about an hour."

Both of her eyebrows nearly jumped off her face. "Uh, where are you going?"

"I have to stop by the Underground." I held her gaze,

knowing she was going to rip me into pieces.

She tossed her purse aside and stood upright, showing her furious gaze. "Why are you going there?" She crossed her arms over her chest, her attitude completely inhospitable. "I thought we were leaving?"

"I just need to take care of something. I'll be back before you know it."

"But what?" she demanded. "Are you buying someone?"

Times like this made me miss my old life, a life where I didn't have to answer to anyone. But her concern also turned me on at the same time. Anytime I was in a dangerous situation, she was worried sick to her stomach. "No. I just need to get some information on someone. Once it's taken care of, we'll leave."

"Who?" she asked. "Why?"

"We'll talk about it later."

"Can I come along?"

That was the dumbest question I'd ever heard. "No."

"Then that means it's dangerous. I thought we were leaving for a nice trip. And now you're telling me you have to go back there..." Her voice broke, and she covered her face with her hands. She slowly dragged them down until she revealed her face again, which was under control once more. But her eyes gave away her anguish.

I was hard just from looking at her. She used to hate

me, and now this was killing her. I was walking into the monster's den, and she could barely stay calm. "I'll be fine, Muse. Like I said, I'll be back before you know it."

She released a deeper sigh, a sigh full of her pain. "Then why won't you tell me what's going on?"

"Because I don't have time. We'll talk later." I turned back to the elevator, knowing this conversation wouldn't stop unless I walked away. It would just spin in circles indefinitely. I hit the button and watched the doors open again.

"An hour?"

I kept the doors open with one arm, then turned around to face her. I stared at the fear in her eyes, the way her arms tightened over her chest like pieces of armor. "An hour."

"You better keep your word, Conway."

"I always do."

THE UNDERGROUND WAS PACKED WITH MEN THAT night, a bunch of assholes looking for a new victim to rape and torture. It was getting harder for me to walk into this place now because I kept picturing what would have happened to Muse if I hadn't been there that night.

If I hadn't saved her.

I could barely swallow because my throat turned so dry.

Bones wasn't there.

That made this easier.

Before Cynthia made it to the table, I walked up to the bar. Men were gathered at the tables, smoking their cigars and drinking brandy. Iron was talking to them, laughing uproariously when one of the psychopaths said something funny.

"You look tired." Cynthia stopped in front of me at the counter, her tits out like usual. She only wore a thong when she worked the tables, and she walked out of there every night with more tips than any waitress could ever dream of.

"Because I am." I should be on a plane right now. I should be with the woman who was waiting for me. But I was there, standing in the shadows where I didn't belong. "Scotch on the rocks."

She started to make the drink. "You know, I always come to your table."

"I guess I'm in a hurry tonight."

She pulled out two cigars and set them on the counter.

I held up my hand. "I don't smoke anymore."

She smiled. "Sounds like you have a woman in your life, then."

I didn't smile or give any indication that she was right.

"I need you to do something for me."

She finished the drink and slid it toward me. "I'm not for sale. I just make the drinks."

"Not what I'm interested in." There was only one pussy I wanted to fuck these days.

"I'm listening..."

"I've got ten thousand euros for you...if you get some info for me."

She glanced at the men, who were busy talking amongst themselves. Iron wasn't paying attention. Her gaze shifted back to me. "What kinda of info?"

"There's a man that comes in here sometimes...his name is Bones. You know him?"

She grabbed the rag and pretended to wipe down the counter, making herself look busy. "Yeah, I know him."

"What can you tell me about him?"

"He's not a guy I cross. It's gonna cost more than ten to get me to talk."

"Fifteen?" I countered.

"Twenty."

That was still change to me, so I just accepted it. "Fine."

"What do you want to know?"

"Is he descended from Bones? The arms dealer in Rome from about thirty years ago."

Her eyes narrowed as she absorbed the information.

"Strange question."

"Just want to know where he comes from. Why is his name Bones?"

"I always thought it was because he likes to break the bones of his victims before he kills them."

"Well, I need a more concrete answer than that. Can you get that for me?"

She eyed the men as she considered it. "I'll have to ask him next time he's in here."

"I know."

"And this is riskier. It's gonna take forty now."

Man, this woman could negotiate. "Done." I grabbed the napkin and scribbled my number down. "Call me when you have the answer."

She grabbed it and tucked it underneath the counter. "You got it."

I left the cash on the table and made my way to a seat.

A few minutes later, the auction started. There were five women on the stage that night, and one woman caught my attention.

Because she wasn't a woman.

She was just a girl.

Young, like Yasmine. She was way too young and innocent to be here. Tears streamed down her face, and her naked body showed the signs of early adulthood. She'd probably had her first period just a few years ago.

I bid on the other women but made sure I didn't win. I was just there to blend in and then disappear. Muse was waiting for me, and I didn't want to make her wait longer than I had to.

But then the young girl was auctioned off.

And the monsters descended.

"Ten million," Iron said at the podium. "Do I have twelve?"

A man in a suit raised his paddle.

"Twenty," a man from the corner said.

"I've got twenty," Iron said. "Any—"

"Twenty-five," another man said.

Shit. Every man in that room wanted to fuck this girl, to break her until her spirit was long gone. They wanted to ruin her innocence, to destroy her completely.

It was disgusting.

"Twenty-five million," Iron said. "Going once... Going twice..."

Dammit. I raised my paddle. "Thirty."

"Thirty million," Iron said.

No one else raised their paddles.

"Sold to Mr. Barsetti." Iron smacked his mallet against the podium. "Congratulations."

I GOT THE GIRL INTO THE CAR, ALL OF OUR LUGGAGE sitting in the backseat. I had to give her some of Muse's clothes because she had nothing to wear. I drove out of Milan and headed to Carter's because I didn't know where else to go. I couldn't keep her, obviously. "What's your name?"

She didn't answer. She pressed her entire body against the window and started to shiver.

"I'm not going to hurt you. I'm going to get you back home, alright?"

She just stared at me.

I called Carter over the sound system.

"What?" Carter said when he picked up. "How'd it go?"

"Cynthia is gonna question Bones next time he comes in. But that's not why I'm calling."

"I was hoping I'd get an invite on your yacht," he teased.

I chuckled. "No way in hell, man."

"Hey, we've taken trips together before."

When we were picking up women left and right and fucking them all over the place. "There was a young girl in the lineup tonight. Even younger than Yasmine."

"Sick fucks."

"They were fighting over her like a piece of meat...so I bought her."

"Seriously?" he snapped. "You're joking, right?"

"No...she's in the car with me."

"I'm not splitting that shit with you. She's not on the list."

"I know...but I couldn't let them have her." She was way too young to die that way. She wasn't a cheap purchase, and I would never get that money back, but I wouldn't be able to sleep that night knowing I did nothing to help her. "So, I'm dropping her off at your place. I'll be there in twenty minutes."

"Uh, excuse me?" he snapped. "I've got company."

"Pull your pants up and send her home. You've got work to do."

He growled into the phone. "I just got rid of Yasmine."

"Then you have room for one more."

"Hey, you're the one who bought her. This is your problem."

"Shut up, Carter. I'm dropping her off."

He sighed. "Fine. But you owe me for this."

"Asshole, you owe me for a lot of shit too." I hung up.

AFTER I DROPPED HER OFF, I HEADED BACK TO MILAN where Muse was waiting for me. It would take me an extra forty-five minutes just to get back.

I broke my promise. I'd been gone two hours.

I knew she didn't contact me because she was too afraid to. Maybe she thought sending me a text would set my phone off and incriminate me somehow. So, I called her through the speakers in the car.

She picked up before the first ring ended. "Are you alright?"

"I'm fine, Muse. I just left Verona, so it'll be about forty-five minutes before I'm back."

"You said it would be one hour."

"I know... I'm sorry." In my former life, I would tell her to get over it. But now, I actually felt like I owed her an explanation. I told her I would come back to her, and when I didn't, I felt like I let her down.

"But you're okay?" she whispered.

"Yes. Completely."

"What happened?"

I drove through the countryside, wrapped up in darkness. Only the light from dashboard gave any illumination. "I'll tell you when I get back."

"No, you're going to tell me now. You've got forty-five minutes."

I couldn't help but smile at the authority in her voice. She knew she had power over me. She just didn't abuse it often. "I told you how my aunt died a while back."

"Yes..."

"I told you some man named Bones killed her."

"Yes," she whispered.

"Last time I went to the Underground, there was a man named Bones there. Young, good-looking, arrogant... I knew he wasn't the original Bones. He's been dead for thirty years, and even if he weren't, he'd been in his sixties by now. But there's no way this guy's name is a coincidence. It means something... I'm just not sure what it is."

She breathed into the phone.

"So, I went to the Underground tonight and asked the waitress to do some digging for me. I paid her for the information, and she'll call me once she has it. That's all I wanted tonight, so once the auction was over, I was going to head back to the apartment. But there was this girl..." My hand tightened into a fist on the steering wheel. It was dark, so I couldn't see my skin, but I knew my knuckles were turning white. "She was so young, Muse. I'm talking...maybe fourteen."

"God..." She sighed into the phone.

"I was going to leave the second the auction was over, but then all the men started fighting over her... It was disgusting. So I bought her instead."

"Conway..."

"I just dropped her off at Carter's. Now I'm back on the road coming to you."

"That was..." She never finished her sentence.

"She cost a lot, but I wouldn't have been able to sleep tonight if I hadn't done anything. None of those women deserve that fate, but this girl is still a kid. She had no idea what was going in. She wouldn't even talk to me in the car. She was so scared."

A quiet sniff escaped across the phone. "You did the right thing..."

In my life, there was no right or wrong. There was just instinct. And my instinct told me to get that girl out of there.

"You're such a good man, Conway."

Normally, I would disagree with her. I would tell her to never say that again. But this time, I didn't. This time, I relished the way it felt on my ears. I didn't drop thirty million dollars for Muse's sake. I wasn't looking for approval or glory. I just did it because I wanted to, not because of the way Muse would feel about me.

We didn't say anything else. The silence stretched across the line as I kept driving. Just as if we were sitting across from each other at breakfast, we didn't make small talk. I could have just hung up, but I didn't want to. I loved the heavy silence between us, the connection that still bound us even miles apart.

I could feel her.

She could feel me.

8

SAPPHIRE

I'D SEEN PICTURES OF GREECE ONLINE, THE TALL WHITE buildings with the dark blue domes as the roof. I'd seen pictures of the Mediterranean, manipulated to look brighter and bluer. But none of those images did justice to reality.

It was breathtaking.

Sailboats were along the edge of the island, floating across the Mediterranean looking for seafood. The white color of their hulls was bright under the unforgiving sun. The city stretched backward up the hill, growing taller as the buildings reached the center of the island.

I stood on the back patio of his villa, a beautiful white building that had its own access to the harbor where his yacht was parked. Luxurious and big, it was designed in the same style as the rest of Santorini. There was a large pool that overlooked the blue sea and a nice balcony that could take in the stunning views.

I stood on the porch with my arms crossed over my chest, unable to absorb what I was looking at.

Conway put our bags away inside the house, used to the sight because he'd seen it so many times.

But for someone like me, this was a once-in-a-lifetime experience. "Oh. My. God."

Conway came up behind me and wrapped his arms around my waist. "What do you think?"

"What do I think?" I asked incredulously. "It's gorgeous. I don't even understand what I'm looking at right now. How can the world be this beautiful?"

He smothered my neck with kisses, his warm breaths falling across my skin. "I've seen something else more beautiful..."

I tilted my neck to give him more access as my lips rose in a smile. I gripped his forearms and enjoyed his kisses while I looked out into the beauty of the Greek island right before me. Pictures didn't do this place justice. "What do we do first?"

"What would you like to do?"

"I don't know... I want to swim in the pool, but I also want to stick my feet in the ocean. But then I'm also hungry. And I want to explore the town...and sail on your yacht. I can't decide."

He chuckled against my ear. "I'll have dinner delivered, and we'll sit in the pool as the sun goes down. How about that?"

"Perfect."

We sat in the pool together with our wineglasses on the deck. The sun was gone, but the lights from the curvature of the island could be seen. The warmth had dissipated, but there was still humidity in the air.

I sat beside him in the water, looking out into a view I couldn't describe.

Conway moved me onto his lap, adjusting me easily because I was buoyant in the water. "Did you enjoy your dinner?"

"It was the best lobster I've ever had...and one of the few I've ever had."

He grinned slightly, his hard chest reflecting the blue light from the pool. His arm scooped under my legs behind my knees, and he rubbed his nose against mine. "You can eat lobster every day if you want."

"No, I'm eating light tomorrow. I ate way too much today."

His hand moved over my stomach. "Really? Because I think you're perfect."

My arms surrounded his neck. "You're a lingerie designer. I need to be a hundred pounds or less."

"For the runway. But you aren't a model. You're just mine now." He rubbed his nose against my cheek. "And I like you well fed and happy. You're sexy no matter what your size."

I chuckled. "You know every woman in the world wants to hear that."

"And it looks like you get to listen to it."

"Because I'm insanely lucky," I said with a laugh. After the words jumped out of my throat, I realized what I'd said and how stupid it was to say it. But I brushed it off and looked into the water, pretending it never happened.

He rested his face against the side of my cheek, his fingers grazing across my thigh under the water.

I sat still, letting the ocean breeze move over the dry skin of my shoulders. "Have you brought other women here?"

"Is that really a conversation you want to have?"

I stared at our bodies under the water, feeling his warm breath graze across my skin. "I guess I'm just curious."

"I've never brought a woman here before, no. But I've met women while I've been here."

So, I was the only company that he took on his

vacations. That still made me feel special—in a way. "What are we going to do tomorrow?"

"We can take the yacht, or we can walk around in Oia."

"Is Oia the town?"

"Yes. It's just a walkway where there are no cars. It's quaint and cute."

"That does sound nice."

"So, would you like to do that?"

"I've never had a choice before. And now I get to decide things. It's interesting."

"You've always had a choice, Muse. It just took you a while to figure it out." His hand moved up my back, and he pulled the string of my bikini, making my top come loose and then slip into the pool. His hands moved for my bottoms next, sliding them over my hips and down my thighs under the water.

Once I was naked under the water, he pulled on his drawstring and loosened his trunks. He slipped them off and set them on the deck. Despite the coolness of the water, his dick was long and hard.

I thought he wanted me on his lap, so I straddled his hips and felt his hard cock rub against my aching clit. I was turned on without even realizing it. Or perhaps my body was ready to go at any time when it came to Conway Barsetti.

He carried me into deeper water and then pressed my back against the wall. He gathered my legs around his waist and then slipped his dick into my slit, finding more resistance than usual in the beginning before he was completely inside me.

I locked my arms around his neck and pressed my face close to his, moaning at his large size. No matter how many times he took me, it always felt like a new experience. My thighs squeezed his hips, and I panted against his lips. He hadn't even started to move yet and I was shaking.

He didn't kiss me. Instead, he watched my face as he rocked into me and pressed me against the wall.

I stared back at him, watching him watch me. "Conway…"

He released a quiet moan under his breath. "Muse."

I held on to him as we moved slowly, his dick sliding through my slickness at a slow pace. The water didn't shift around us with his movements because everything was so slow. It was about the combining of our bodies, not the speed of our movements. "I like it when you make love to me like this…"

He slid his entire length inside me and then paused, letting his fat dick stretch me wide apart. He paused for emphasis, to remind me that he had all of me, every single inch that he could claim. "I do too."

We spent the morning shopping in the town, getting coffees, and then exploring the Atlantis Book Store. The cobblestone streets showed panoramic views of the rest of Santorini, and every time I looked at my surroundings, I could hardly believe we were there.

It was so beautiful.

Conway kept me close to him everywhere we went, his arm around my waist or in my hair when he kissed me outside the shop. He told me to buy whatever I wanted, and that didn't just apply to our trip.

We had lunch at a small café before we walked back to his villa near the water. Then we packed for the yacht and set sail in the Mediterranean. Conway didn't need a captain because he could handle everything on his own. He moved out of the harbor and into the open sea, keeping the sights of Santorini in the background.

I sat in the front and stared at the jagged rocks that stuck up out of the water. A sunhat covered my face and shoulders, but there was no real way to escape the hot sun. I sat in my bikini, enjoying the scorching day.

Conway turned off the engine and let the yacht sit on the waves. We rocked up and down, but the water was fairly calm, protected by the rocky outcroppings that surrounded us in the sea.

He sat beside me in the cushioned seat, his arm moved around my shoulders. Shirtless with sunglasses sitting on the bridge of his nose, he looked like he was made for a vacation like this. Handsome with tanned skin, he blended in with the Greek island perfectly.

"It's beautiful out here."

"I know." His fingertips glided up and down my arm.

"Have you thought about work since we got here?"

His hand paused. "Actually, no."

"That's good. This place brings out the best in you."

"I love Verona. It's peaceful and beautiful. But I love it here too. My heart is torn in two pieces."

"Since you work remotely, you should spend more time here."

He shook his head slightly. "I need all of my supplies. It would be difficult to transfer that here. And there're a lot of things that just need to be handled in person. I could make it work in Tuscany if I had to, but here, it would be too difficult."

My face slightly turned his way. "So, you think about moving back?"

He shrugged. "It crosses my mind sometimes."

His parents would be so happy if he really relocated to Tuscany. They loved him so much, wore their hearts on their sleeves constantly. "Thank you for bringing me here. I'll never forget it…"

His fingers moved under the fall of my hair and gently played with my strands. "I've enjoying having you, Muse. No one else I'd rather be here with."

Our relationship had changed in the last month. I felt a deeper connection to him, a kind of affection that burned deep inside our hearts. I'd grown attached to him, cared about him so much that I couldn't function when I thought he might be in danger. But it seemed like I felt the same emotions from him, the same fondness.

He said there was no future for us.

But what if he changed his mind?

What if there was something here?

Time seemed to stand still as we enjoyed our time at his villa. We spent our days sailing, eating, fucking, and doing absolutely nothing. Days had gone by, but it happened so fast it seemed like only minutes had passed.

I loved living in Verona, but Santorini had a special quality to it.

Night had deepened, so we sat on the couch together and watched TV. His arm was around my shoulders, and he was wearing just his sweatpants, his hard chest warm. His fingers played with my hair, and the lights from the harbor could be seen through the window.

I rested my head on his shoulder and closed my eyes, feeling a wave of peace.

I never wanted to leave. "Can we stay here forever?"

He chuckled. "As tempting as that sounds, no."

"I like it when you don't work."

"Me too," he said. "But it can't last forever."

"Do you ever think about retiring? You're so successful that you could if you wanted to."

"I don't believe in retirement," he said. "Once you stop having a purpose, you lose your mind. I'll probably work until the day I die."

"If that's the case, maybe you shouldn't work so hard."

He looked down at me, a smile on his face. "You have a point there."

"You have the ability to travel the world. So why don't you do that more?"

"I've been to a lot of places."

"But have you been everywhere?" I questioned.

His smile stretched wider. "Is this your way of getting me to take you around the world? Because if that's what you want, just ask."

"Does that mean you would take me?"

He rubbed his nose against mine. "You know I would give you anything you asked for."

My hand moved up his chest, and I felt my heart soften like melted butter. This man was nothing like he used to be. He had been cold, rude, and insulting. But now he treated me like a goddess, did anything to make me happy.

He loved me.

He never said it, but that didn't make it untrue. Whether he wanted to admit it out loud or not, it didn't change reality.

He loved me. "Conway—"

His phone started ringing on the coffee table. He glanced down at the screen. When his eyes narrowed, I knew it was important. "I'm sorry, Muse. I have to take this." He pressed the phone to his ear and walked into the other room. "It's Conway." He stopped in front of the window overlooking the patio and listened to whatever was said over the line.

I stared at his muscular physique, studied the sculpted muscles of his torso and his shoulders. He was a perfect specimen of masculinity, a statue that could be placed in the streets of Greece. He was the kind of man women dreamed of having.

He rubbed the back of his neck and kept listening. "You're certain? Absolutely?" He listened again. "Thank you, Cynthia." He hung up and dropped the phone into his pocket. His arms slowly crossed over his chest as he looked into the darkness outside the window.

"What is it?" My bare feet padded against the hardwood floor as I approached him, staring at the tight muscles of his back. Maybe it was none of my business and I shouldn't pry, but my curiosity couldn't be controlled.

He didn't answer, his forearms appearing more corded than usual. "That was the waitress at the Underground."

I stood at his side, seeing the way his jaw tightened with snapping force. It was impossible to read him at that moment, to understand if that was bad news or really bad news. "And?"

He rubbed his fingers along his jawline, his eyes wide open because he hadn't blinked once since he got off the phone. "It's exactly what I feared."

9
CONWAY

CARTER STEPPED INSIDE MY STUDY AND SAT ON THE couch across from me. His drink was already sitting there, the ice cubes fresh and the glass frosty. My elbows rested on my knees, and my fingertips rested against my mouth.

I didn't look at him, my mind still reeling from the way my world had just shifted.

He took a deep drink before setting the glass on the cherry wood, making a thud and leaving a water ring. "How was your trip?"

"Not here to talk about that."

"I know. I just thought we could have a good conversation before we have the bad one." He took another drink.

The lights were low, and the sun had set hours ago. Muse and I returned to Italy shortly after my conversation with Cynthia. I had a great time, but once I knew the truth, I couldn't enjoy myself any longer. "It was too short."

"You were there for five days?"

Felt like five minutes. "Yeah."

He sat back against the cushion and rested his ankle on the opposite knee. In jeans and a t-shirt, he was casual since it was past five in the evening. "I sent that girl home. I could barely get a few words out of her."

"Good. I'm glad she's where she belongs."

"She gave me her name and her home address. But other than that, she was dead silent the entire time."

"Understandable."

"But she did want me to tell you that she said thank you."

My eyes shifted to the floor, and I tried not to feel good about what I did. Muse thought my actions were selfless, but I considered it an act of redemption. Doing one right thing didn't fix all my wrongs...but it helped. "I hope she'll be more careful next time."

"I'm sure she won't leave the house now. And her family will probably relocate." He grabbed his drink and finished it. The decanter of brandy was on the coffee table, so he refilled his glass. "I know why you called me here tonight. I know why you cut your trip short. So just tell me what I don't want to hear."

My eyes moved to his face, and my frown deepened.

"His mother was pregnant with him when his father was killed by our family. His middle name is Bones, but that's the name he prefers to go by."

"Shit." He ran his fingers through his hair, his shoulders slouching in disappointment. "And you're certain?"

I nodded. "The story checks out."

"What's his first and last name?"

"No idea. He didn't tell her, and she didn't want to make it obvious by asking."

"I wonder if we can find that information on our own."

"Probably."

"What do we do?" he asked. "He's had plenty of time to hit us but never has. Maybe he's left the past where it belongs."

"Maybe. Maybe not. I don't think we can take that chance."

"You're right. We can't."

"We have to talk to our fathers about it."

He dragged his hands down his face and sighed. "Yeah, you're right."

"You want to drive there tomorrow?"

"I guess," he said. "I've got shit to do, but I guess it can wait."

"It has to wait."

He finished his drink in one go. "They're gonna break our arms."

"Probably."

"And leave a few dents in our skulls."

"More than likely."

"I would normally say we deserve it, but now, I'm not so sure. If we weren't part of the Underground, how would we have even known about it? If it weren't for us, we wouldn't even know Bones had a son."

"I don't think they'll see it that way." My father respected me as a man, but he would always be a little protective of me.

"And our mothers… Oh man."

"We'll definitely get slapped."

"The only time I like getting slapped is when a gorgeous woman in on my lap…"

That made two of us. "We'll leave tomorrow and hope for the best."

"Alright. Tomorrow. Are you bringing Sapphire?"

I didn't want her to be part of this. I didn't want her to worry about the shit that really happened in this cruel world. "No. She's staying here."

WHEN I WOKE THE NEXT MORNING, I PACKED MY

things into a bag, careful not to wake Muse. I wouldn't leave without saying goodbye, but the second she watched me pack, she would know I wouldn't be sticking around.

When I finished, I pulled the zipper up.

And that's what made her stir. She reached beside her as she searched for me on the bed. When I wasn't there, she opened her eyes and looked around the room. Her eyes settled on me, and an instant look of relief came into her gaze.

It made me feel good and shitty at the same time.

She sat up, running her fingers through her long hair. "Morning."

"Morning." I moved to the edge of the bed to kiss her.

Her lips moved with mine gently, giving me more than just a quick peck on the lips. It was a warm greeting, sensual and sexy.

It made me want to stay.

When I pulled away, she noticed my duffel bag on the edge of the bed. It only took her a few seconds to process what was happening. I was already dressed to leave, and it was barely seven in the morning. "What's going on?"

"Carter and I are going to Tuscany for a few days. We need to have a conversation with our fathers about what's going on."

"And why doesn't this trip include me?"

There would be too much going on for me to babysit

her. And I didn't want to scare her, to have her see my family's anger. "I think it's best if you stay here. It'll only be a few days."

"A few days is a lifetime."

"Invite Vanessa over."

"You know that's not why I want to come, Conway." She stared at me with those piercing eyes, the emotion turbulent. She moved to her knees and sat on the balls of her feet, my t-shirt fitting her like a loose blanket. "Where you go, I go."

We'd become inseparable over the last few months. She used to be my prisoner, but now she'd become my friend, my confidant, and my mistress. Our lives joined together in the most unpredictable way, and now we were practically a single person. Whenever I wasn't by her side, she worried about me.

I had a woman who worried about me.

"It's just not appropriate, Muse. Not this time."

Her eyes lit up with frustration, but she didn't argue against me. She kept her anger at bay. "You've told me about this guy already. It's not like I don't understand what's going on."

It was still a conversation for the men, not the women. "No."

"I could at least stay at—"

"I'm not going to change my mind, Muse. You know I

take you wherever I go. But this time, it's just not appropriate. My father will be angry. My mother will be furious. My uncle and aunt will be upset... It's not going to be a nice family get-together like you're used to seeing. My family knows how to celebrate and live life to the fullest, but just like everyone else, we've got our baggage. This is one of those times. I need to do this by myself."

She released a quiet sigh, and her eyes slowly started to relax.

"I'll be back in a few days. It'll be over before you know it."

"Are you leaving right now?" she whispered.

"Yes."

She rose onto her knees and moved her fingertips underneath my t-shirt to my torso. She felt the grooves of my abs as she drifted farther up. "Do you have a few minutes?" The pleading gaze in her eyes pierced right through my skin.

My woman wanted me between her legs.

And I wasn't going to refuse her. "I always have a few minutes for you."

CARTER DROVE WHILE I SAT IN THE PASSENGER SEAT. We spent most of the drive in silence with the radio on to fill the emptiness. Like with Muse, Carter and I were close enough that the quiet didn't make either of us uncomfortable. We could exist together for hours without carrying on a conversation.

But in this instance, the silence was strained. We were both thinking the same thing, dreading the same thing.

Carter turned down the radio, the preamble to conversation. "I know I give you shit about it, but I'm being serious now. What's the rundown with you and Sapphire? Is this the real deal now?"

I kept my gaze focused out the passenger window. "We've never talked about women before. Let's not start now."

"Never talk about it?" he asked incredulously. "That's all we ever talk about."

"You know what I mean."

"Then that implies Sapphire isn't like the other women we talk about, the women we pick up and brag about."

"You're right," I said quietly. "She's not."

"So, then she is the real deal?"

I only gave him my silence.

"I'm not asking you to be a nosy prick. I'm asking because we're family." He glanced at me every few minutes, but his eyes were glued to the road most of the time. "Our whole family loves Sapphire. They can't get enough of her. You've given her your freedom. You shower her with affection in the public eye. And now you're taking lavish trips with her."

I still didn't speak.

"I guess that's the most confirmation I'm going to get."

When it came to Muse, I didn't know how to describe what we had. I wanted to say she was just some woman I was fucking, but everyone knew that wasn't the case. Even I knew that wasn't the case. But I wouldn't go so far as to say she was my girlfriend...even though that's exactly what she seemed.

But a future still wasn't on the table. I would grow bored of her eventually, and my tastes would change. My desires would shift, and so would my designs. There was nothing sexy about marriage or parenthood. I could never let Muse be anything more than a mistress.

"For what it's worth," Carter said. "I really like her."

"You don't even know her, Carter."

"I don't need to know her. She makes you happy—and that's all that matters."

We arrived in Tuscany, driving through the golden fields and eyeing the endless vineyards. Ruined castles dotted the remote land, and on a clear day like this, Florence could be seen in the distance.

"It's time to make the call," Carter said.

I pulled out my phone and stared at my father's name

before dialing. I was dreading this, but the dread would only increase the longer I procrastinated.

My father answered almost immediately. "Hey, son. How are you?"

Pretty shitty. "Good. Carter and I are on the road, and we're thirty minutes from the house."

My father paused for a while. "I didn't know you were stopping by. What a nice surprise."

It wouldn't be that nice pretty soon. "Carter and I need to talk to you and Uncle Cane. And we should talk somewhere in private…"

Another pause endured, but this one much longer than before. He didn't ask any questions like most people would. He had the patience of a monk. A sigh didn't erupt over the phone. "Cane and I will meet you there. Should your mother be involved?"

"Definitely not."

"We'll meet you soon."

MY FATHER'S OFFICE WAS ONE OF THE ROOMS IN THE house I hardly visited growing up. I was told to stay out of it, and even as I got older, that rule never changed. Now that I sat there on the couch with Carter beside me, I understood why.

Lady in Lingerie

My dad had enough scotch to last an apocalypse.

The fireplace was empty because it hadn't been used in three months. His dark desk seemed just as untouched. He had two couches that faced each other, and on the walls were peculiar paintings constructed of buttons.

Is that why he called my mother Button? Did she make those?

My father poured four glasses of scotch and sat with Uncle Cane. The four of us faced each other, and my father and Uncle Cane stared us down with a silent coldness. Like they were meeting an enemy rather than their own family, they were harsh.

"Be straight." My father brought his hands together with his elbows resting on his knees.

"Spit it out," Uncle Cane said. "Or we'll drag it out."

I felt like a young boy again, being disciplined by my guardians. Most parents wanted to be the only ones who disciplined their children, but my father and uncle were different. My uncle had been a second father to me. If I acted out of line, he didn't hesitate before giving me a good smack. My father did the same to Carter. "I'll start with the important information and work backward."

"Alright," my father said. "What is it?"

I didn't want to say his name out loud because I knew how much it angered my father. My father didn't talk about the past very often, and that was for a reason. He lived through more than I knew, and I could see the pain behind his eyes anytime the past was mentioned. "Bones has a son."

My father tensed slightly, his eyes narrowing even more than before.

Uncle Cane was a lot more transparent. Both of his hands automatically tightened into fists.

"He's our age, give or take a few years," Carter said. "His mother was pregnant when the older Bones died. She named her son after him, at least, made Bones his middle name."

"But that's the name he goes by now," I said. "That's what he calls himself. He's covered in tattoos, he's arrogant, and he's associated with the Underground. He knows the Skull Kings, and anytime we've asked someone about him, there's fear in their eyes. Once we confirmed he really was who we thought he was, we knew we had to tell you."

My father looked at Uncle Cane.

Uncle Cane stared back.

The silence stretched, becoming heavier with every passing second.

My father spoke first. "I want to know how you even crossed paths with him. How do you know who the Skull Kings are, and how did you find the Underground? But I suspect ignorance is better at this point...so I don't murder my own son."

As much as I wanted to look away, I didn't. I held his gaze, seeing the fierce disappointment in his expression. It hurt. It hurt so much that I wished he would just punch me in the face instead. An apology would fit right about now, but I knew they were just empty words to him.

"And mine," Uncle Cane added.

Carter held his father's gaze, but I knew he felt like shit just the way I did.

"Fuck it." Uncle Cane rose off the sofa and helped himself to my father's desk. He pulled out two cigars, lit them, and then handed one to my father.

My father didn't hesitate before he took it.

"Booze isn't gonna cut it this time." Uncle Cane sat down again, sucking on the tip of the cigar like it was air rather than smoky ash.

"You've been lying to me." My father stared me down, his hard jaw sharp enough to cut through glass. "My own son has been lying to me." He didn't raise his voice, but his tone was still deadly. He didn't need to drop a single curse word to be more intimidating.

"I didn't lie—"

"Just because you're a grown man doesn't mean I won't knock your teeth out. I don't give a damn if you're a famous billionaire."

I clenched my jaw and stayed quiet. Only my father could talk to me that way and get away with it.

Uncle Cane was just as angry, but he pushed the conversation forward. "Start from the beginning."

The beginning started a long time ago. Carter and I had been doing this for years.

"I'll give you the short version of the long version," Carter began. "Conway and I have been buying women from the Underground for years now. The Skull Kings take women from affluent families, from people who've wronged someone else. It's an act of revenge. The families of the victims contact me. They offer a price, and once we negotiate the right deal, Conway goes to the Underground and buys them. We put the girls in his lingerie shows for a short period of time, and then they're returned to the families."

My father pieced it together quickly. "You make a profit from rescuing them."

It was the only time I wanted to close my eyes because I couldn't stand his disappointment. "Yes…"

"How much money have you made doing this?" Uncle Cane asked.

"Doesn't matter," Carter said.

"Yes, it does fucking matter," Uncle Cane snapped.

"How I earn my money is none of your business," Carter countered. "I'm a grown man. I get you're pissed at me because of this whole thing, but that doesn't give you the right to cross the line."

Uncle Cane looked like he might break Carter's neck.

"We've been doing it for a long time," I continued. "That's why we're at the Underground often. And that's when I encountered Bones. I heard someone say his name, and I recognized it right away. I did some digging...and found out who he was."

"Does he know who you are?" my father asked, calm and livid at the same time.

"Yes," I answered. "One of the Skull Kings said my name in front of him."

"What was his response?" Uncle Cane asked.

"He didn't have much of a response," I replied. "He didn't react at all."

My father stared at me coldly, considering everything I said in silence.

Uncle Cane did the same.

"We didn't want to talk about this," Carter said. "And we wouldn't have unless we thought it was important. We thought you should know about Bones. Whether he's a threat or not, that remains to be determined."

"Always assume that he is." Uncle Cane took another long drag of his cigar, letting the smoke out through his nostrils.

I could go for a cigar right now, but my loyalty to Muse forbade it.

My father didn't say anything else, and neither did

Uncle Cane. Our glasses were untouched in front of us. The silence became thicker and thicker. Heat burned my neck, and the tension made me sick to my stomach.

I thought we would discuss what our next move was, but our fathers were silent.

"Where should we start?" I asked.

My father inhaled his cigar before dropping it into the ashtray. "Get out, Conway." My father didn't look at me as he dismissed us. "We'll finish this conversation tomorrow."

I exchanged a look with Carter, knowing our fathers wanted to talk in private. They were both too pissed to talk tactics.

"Go," Uncle Cane said. "And you can make your own arrangements for the evening."

It was the first time I wasn't welcome in the house.

That probably stung most of all.

Carter and I left the office and walked downstairs toward the entryway. My mother was in the dining room, so she heard us as we made our way to the front door. Her eyes were still full of adoration, looking at me like she couldn't love me more than she already did. "Leaving?"

I wanted to enjoy that look a little longer before she became cold like my father. She would be just as disappointed, just as livid. Instead of greeting me with a hug and a kiss on the cheek, her palm would slap against my face. "Good night, Mother." I walked out before she could hold me back.

"Conway."

I couldn't walk away from my mother when she was talking to me, so I turned around.

"You aren't staying?" she asked sadly.

My childhood home was no longer open to me. The gates were locked, and I didn't have a key. My father didn't want to look at me anymore, and my mother would feel the same way once my father told her the truth. "No."

CARTER AND I SAT IN A BAR TOGETHER IN FLORENCE, drinking scotch while we faced each other in the booth. We hadn't spoken on the drive, and we still hadn't spoken in the last fifteen minutes.

We just kept drinking.

Carter lit up a cigar and let the smoke slowly drift from his mouth to the ceiling. He switched between the booze and the cigar, two of the most important things to a man. The third was women.

I'd cut smoking out of my life, so I just stuck to the booze.

Carter finally broke the silence. "That went well..."

I knew exactly how it was going to play out, but facing my father's real-life disappointment stung. "Yeah."

"I've never been kicked out of the house before, not even when my dad caught me having a threesome with those two girls in high school."

My father had never kicked me out either. "It's pretty shitty."

"I don't think it makes us terrible people, but I feel like I'm on trial."

"I think they're just angry with us for getting mixed up in dangerous bullshit."

"Like they've never gotten mixed up in dangerous bullshit," he spat.

"They won't see it that way."

"They're going to tell us to stop going to the Underground."

My father would demand it. "As much as I respect my father, he can't tell me what to do. It's my life. I'll do what I want."

"So, you're still in?"

Now I wasn't in it for the money anymore. I felt obligated to keep going. Without me, these women would have no chance. If I hadn't been at the Underground that night, what would have happened to Muse? She would be dead right now.

My woman would be dead.

"I don't know," I answered. "My point is, they can't control what we do. I hate feeling his wrath and his disappointment, but I'm not sorry for what I did."

"I'm not either."

"So, we'll just have to deal with it. Hopefully, we can get to work tomorrow. They can only be mad at us for so long."

"True."

We finished our drinks, paid the tab, and then walked to our hotel. We were staying at the Hotel Firenze Four Seasons, a five-star resort. We walked into the lobby together, said good night, and then went to our rooms.

It didn't matter how nice the suite was. It didn't compare to my old bedroom. And it didn't matter how comfortable the bed was. It was nothing without my woman lying beside me.

I brushed my teeth and washed my face before getting into bed. I couldn't remove the image of my father's face from my head, the tight line of his shadow and the threat in his eyes. He wasn't the most affectionate man, but he blanketed me with love in his own way. But now, all that was replaced by sheer disappointment.

My phone rang on the nightstand, and without looking to see the name on the screen, I knew exactly who it was. I grabbed the phone and realized she was trying to video message me. I took the call and rested my phone upright on my chest so she could see my face. "Hey."

"Is this a bad time?" The video showed her lying in bed on her side, my sheets surrounding her. She wore one of my black t-shirts. With no makeup and her hair wild, she looked exactly as she did every other night.

Beautiful.

"No. Just got into bed."

She stared at me with observant eyes. "It didn't go well."

"I'm sorry."

"I'm sleeping in a hotel tonight."

"Wow… So it *really* didn't go well."

"Yeah. My father is pretty upset with me right now."

"Why?" she asked. "You've saved so many women."

"That's not the whole story, and you know it, Muse. I make money off people's misfortune. If people don't pay, we don't save."

"Not true," she whispered. "You just saved that girl at your own expense."

"That was a one-time thing…"

"Say whatever you want, Con." It was the first time she'd called me that, using an intimate nickname only my family used.

"And he's also angry I put myself in danger."

"Because he loves you."

I watched her on the screen, looking at her just as I would if I were in bed beside her. But if I were really there in person, I'd be between her legs right now. There was nowhere I'd rather be than buried deep inside her. It seemed to make everything better, to make me forget all the bullshit in the world. "I hate it when he looks at me like that."

"It won't last forever."

"But it'll last a long time."

"You should be happy he's upset. If he didn't care about you, he wouldn't be angry. It shows that he cares—that he loves you."

"I still hate it."

"It'll pass..."

Watching her tired features somehow softened my pain. I liked watching her beauty through the screen. I was alone in a hotel room and could beat off to porn, but I'd rather look at her. Gorgeous, exceptional, and affectionate, she was sleeping in my bed, wishing I were there. "How was your day?"

"It was okay. I helped Marco in the stables all day then had dinner. I watched some TV, and now I'm in bed talking to you." She sighed as she turned her head toward the pillow, like talking to me was giving her a sense of peace that helped her drift off to sleep.

"I miss you." The words were yanked out of my mouth

all on their own. I never intended to say them out loud, not when I didn't have a chance to think them. When it came to Muse, everything was instinctual. Blurting out words had become a regular part of my day. I wasn't the affectionate type. I wasn't gentle, kind, or thoughtful. But when it came to this woman, I was a different man.

A very different man.

"I miss you too."

My father wasn't any different the next day.

In fact, he seemed angrier.

We gathered together at the dining table, my father and Uncle Cane on one side, and Carter and I on the other. An invisible line was drawn through the table, dividing us like men across a battlefield.

What surprised me most was when my mother joined us. She took a seat beside my father, her expression hard, as if she knew everything that had been discussed the previous day.

I didn't think this subject was appropriate for her, but I wasn't stupid enough to say that out loud.

Coffee and snacks were on the table, but no one moved to grab anything. The silence was thick like smoke, and it was hard to breathe because it was so harsh on the lungs.

Carter and I didn't speak first, knowing it was smart to let them make the opening statement. If there were a jury in the room, this would look a lot like a trial.

My father finally spoke. "Cane and I did some prodding yesterday. We were able to verify all the information you received. It checks out. His mother was a mistress, not bound by marriage. After Bones died, she had her son seven months later."

"How do we figure out if he's a threat?" I asked. "Should we tail him?"

"No," Uncle Cane answered. "The second Bones died, the boy and his mother disappeared off the grid. They didn't resurface again until a few years ago. He's connected to a lot of people, but it's not clear exactly what he does. But he has strong ties to a lot of groups, ironclad affiliations. The fact that we can't determine his allegiance to anything is both comforting and troublesome."

"Troublesome because we don't know what he believes in," my father added. "He's a powerful man and has had opportunities to hurt us before, but never has. Perhaps he doesn't care to avenge his father and has moved on to better things. After all, he didn't even know him. Since his parents weren't married, I'm sure his mother didn't get a dime of his estate. The blood war could be insignificant to him."

"That would be ideal," I said. "He didn't seem to care that I was sitting directly beside him at the Underground."

"And if he did, do you really think he would act on it?" my father asked coldly.

All I did was stare at him.

"Or maybe he does care," Uncle Cane said. "He's just been waiting for the right time."

"We killed his father because of what he did to our aunt," I said. "It was revenge. Even if he's a psychopath, he must understand that."

My mother immediately looked down. I wouldn't have noticed the movement if my father hadn't glanced at her at the exact same time, as if he expected her to react in some way.

What was I missing?

"He might care," Carter said. "Why else would he name himself Bones? He has some affection for the name."

"But he could just be using the name to his advantage," I said. "Bones was a powerful man. Almost everyone knows that. By adopting that name, he inherits the fear his father once instilled."

"Then should we hit him first?" Carter asked. "Eliminate him before there's a chance to do anything to us?"

"No." My father crossed his arms over his chest. "We do nothing."

"Nothing?" I asked in surprise.

"Nothing," my father repeated. "There's a good chance he doesn't care enough to get in our way. The Barsettis are only known for their wine now. As far as the Underground goes, we're no longer in the criminal business. We sold our business to the Skull Kings. As far as the world can see, we've decided to move on from that life."

"What business?" I asked.

"Yeah," Carter added.

"Not important," my father said. "But if we attempt to attack him first, before he can strike us, we might start another blood war. And that's the last thing we want. We'll keep eyes and ears on him. That's the smartest thing we can do right now."

I wasn't expecting that, but I had to agree with him. Our lives were peaceful now. There was no sense in attacking someone when we had no idea what this man's motives were. Maybe he despised his father.

"But that brings us to our next point," Uncle Cane said. "No more business at the Underground."

"Ever," my father added.

I felt like a ten-year-old child again. My father was disciplining me for doing something stupid. But I wasn't ten anymore. I was almost thirty—and a self-made billionaire. I didn't want to be proud or arrogant, but my father couldn't tell me what to do anymore. "Our business is too important."

"It is," Carter said in agreement. "People depend on us."

"You're taking money from innocent people who just want their daughters back." My father spoke through a clenched jaw, his dark eyes piercing like two blades. "There's nothing noble about your work. You are two cocky idiots who don't know what the hell they're doing. Don't make this about the girls. This is about the money. You're greedy, and worst of all, stupid." Not once did he raise his voice, but his words sank into our skin like blades. "So, it ends now."

Carter fell silent, his eyes trained on his father.

I didn't blink as I stared into the eyes of my biggest hero. "Last time I was there, they were selling a sixteen-year-old girl. I wasn't supposed to buy her, or anyone else. But I dropped thirty million dollars just to get her out of there. Carter put her on a plane back home. Neither one of us made a cent off her. We risked our lives and our necks to get that girl out of there. If that's not brave, I don't know what is."

Instead of softening his expression and being impressed by what I did, it only made him more pissed off. "I didn't go through hell to see my son go down the wrong path. I didn't almost die twice to see my family repeat the same mistakes. Your mother didn't—"

"Crow." My mom silenced him just by saying his name.

And he listened.

"It's my turn to talk now." She moved her hand and rested it on top of his.

He didn't reciprocate the affection, too angry with the world to care about the touch of his wife.

"Conway." She looked at me with soft eyes before looking at my cousin. "Carter. Your fathers are both strong, stubborn, and very protective. Sometimes they seem to exaggerate, but trust me, they don't. You both have accomplished so much in your young lives. Your hearts are in the right place. Whether you're making money off saving these women, it's still a good thing to do. However, you have no idea what you're doing."

Just when I thought my mother would smooth everything over, she threw a curve ball.

"The connections between these men go far deeper than you realize. The Skull Kings have been around much longer than you understand. They were once an assassination crew, taking out leaders, politicians, and anyone who had a big enough bounty on their head. They changed their business into arms dealership, taking over the sector Bones used to hold. Now, they've broken into the trafficking circuit. These men only care about one thing…money. And if they ever find out how much money you've made from selling these women back to where they came from, who will pay the price?"

I held my breath as I listened, hanging on to every word my mother said.

Carter was quiet too.

"Your fathers have worked very hard to give us the simple life we have now. It wasn't always this way. We've all suffered at the hands of madmen in our own ways. We want to put this behind us. So, you must close this door, both of you. As much as you may want to help these women, it's not worth dying for. It's not worth risking your entire family. I know deep down inside your fathers understand. I even believe they're somewhat proud of you. But your actions are directly destroying everything they sacrificed to protect." She turned her gaze on me. "Son."

I took a deep breath as she addressed me.

"I want your promise that you will never participate in the Underground—ever again."

I held her gaze but didn't speak.

She didn't blink. "Conway Barsetti."

I didn't want to hurt my parents. I didn't want to disappoint them. My pride wanted me to remain stubborn and deny them what they wanted. But when my mother spoke so passionately, I couldn't deny her. "I promise."

The air left my father's lungs.

My mom turned to Carter. "Carter, promise all of us that this business is over."

Carter caved quicker than I did. He nodded.

"Out loud," my mom pressed.

"I promise," Carter whispered.

"Now remember, Barsettis always honor their promises," my mother continued. "If you don't, you hurt the family name. And then you won't deserve the honor of the name. So, don't you ever break that vow. Understand?"

My mother reminded me of Muse in some ways. She could command a room even though she was physically the weakest person there. She earned the respect of everyone in different ways. She could make all of us obedient even when she was half our size. "Yes," I answered. "We understand."

10
SAPPHIRE

With Conway was gone, the enormous house felt even bigger.

The sheets were cold against my skin.

The silence of the bedroom was suffocating.

Once upon a time, I couldn't get away from him fast enough.

And now, I couldn't stop missing him.

I finished working in the stables, then headed back to the empty bedroom. I showered but didn't bother putting on makeup since there was no one to impress. My phone rang on the table the second I stepped out of the bathroom. I hoped it was Conway, so I quickly crossed the room and grabbed it.

But it was Vanessa.

The wrong Barsetti. I took the call. "Hey, what's up?"

"Hey," she said cheerfully. "What are you up to tonight?"

"Nothing. Conway is visiting your parents right now, so I'm home alone."

"He is?" she asked in surprise. "Why?"

I knew that information was confidential. "To talk about the show in New York."

Vanessa bought it. "Well, I don't have plans tonight either. Let's go out."

I knew Conway would be weird about that. He didn't like it when I went anywhere alone, especially if he wasn't in the same city. "Or you could come over here. Dante can make dinner, and we can hit the pool."

"Nah," she said. "I want to go out and do something. There's this great place I've been wanting to try close to my apartment."

She just wanted to go to dinner, not head to a club, so that didn't sound so bad. Conway still wouldn't like it, but I might have to ignore him. "Let me see if I can get a ride. I'll let you know."

"Alright."

I hung up then called Conway.

But he didn't answer. It kept ringing until it went to voice mail.

I couldn't recall a single time when I called him and he didn't answer. He must be in the middle of something intense. Even if he were in the middle of a conversation with someone, he would step away. But he must be in a situation where that wasn't an option.

So, I'd have to figure this out on my own.

Conway wouldn't want me to go out alone. That was obvious. But I didn't want to blow Vanessa off, especially since I had nothing else to do for the night. I was lonely and bored, and Vanessa had become a good friend.

So, I had Dante arrange for two of Conway's men to drive me. They would escort me to Milan and then watch me from the vehicle as I had dinner with Vanessa. It would be weird, of course. But when Vanessa asked about it, I could just pin it on Conway.

Because it was believable.

I arrived at the restaurant and found her sitting outside on the patio. She already had a bottle of wine for the table along with two glasses. A fresh basket of bread sat there, still warm and ready to be devoured.

I sat across from her and immediately helped myself to two slices of bread. "This smells delicious…"

"All bread smells delicious. That's the one thing I hate about living here. Bread is an essential part of the diet."

"And you hate that?" I asked incredulously.

"They just make it impossible to cut out carbs."

I rolled my eyes. "Like you need to cut out carbs."

"Believe it or not, I'm skinny because I restrain myself. Unlike men, who can eat whatever they want with no consequences. I went on a date with this guy the other night, and he ate all the bread in the basket by himself—and this guy is ripped."

"Are you going to see him again?"

She sipped her wine then shook her head. "Nah."

"Why?"

"Too clingy. We went out one time, and then he kept texting me all day long. Kept asking when we were going to get together again. It's a shame because he was cute, but it was just too much for me. If I know something isn't going to work out, I think it's best to kill it before it begins to grow, you know?"

"Totally makes sense."

"I didn't want to lead him on and make him even more clingy." She finished her wine before she grabbed the bottle and refilled her glass. "I'm not necessarily looking for Mr. Right, but I'm pretty bummed I haven't met him. There's just not much to choose from. They're either jerks or too suffocating."

Conway was neither of those things. He and I just fit together, despite our unusual beginning.

"When did you know Conway was the one?"

I was about to drink my wine but hesitated when she asked the question. I forced the glass to my lips and took a drink. "I'm surprised you want to know."

"Why? We're friends, right?"

"Yeah, but the guy I'm seeing is your brother."

She shrugged. "I can stop myself from vomiting as long as I have a glass of wine in my hand. So, when did you know?"

There wasn't a specific moment in time when my feelings changed. The process was slow, and my opinion began to change once he showed his softer characteristics. He was protective, loyal, and faithful to me. I guess if I had to choose a defining moment, it was when he decided to let me go. I could stay if I wanted to, or I could leave. But in the end, being with him was the only place I wanted to be.

But I couldn't tell Vanessa that.

"I guess…since the moment I met him."

Vanessa's eyes softened in a way they never had before. "Aww…" She set her glass down, her lips stretching into a beautiful smile. "That's so sweet, even if you are talking about my brother. I always thought he'd want to be with some stuck-up skank with no personality, and I'm so glad he picked you. You're perfect for him."

I smiled back. "Yeah, I think we're perfect together."

Vanessa and I said goodbye on the sidewalk, giving each other a long hug before I turned away and headed to the van.

Out of nowhere, a man walked up with a microphone in his hand. Behind him was a man holding a news crew camera, and judging by the bright red light, the camera was rolling. "Sapphire, can we talk with you for a moment?"

I'd seen paparazzi swarm Conway whenever we went to fashion shows or other events, but I'd never seen them emerge on a quiet evening in the city. I was surprised they were there to begin with. Perhaps other people spotted me and started posting it on the internet.

No wonder Conway didn't want me to go anywhere.

The two men who'd escorted me to Milan got out of the SUV and came toward me, ready to pull me out of the situation and away from the spotlight.

Now I was grateful I'd brought them.

"Is it true that you're living with Conway?" The man turned the microphone to my mouth.

"I... I have to go." I'd already experienced this attention once when I was in New York. But that event still didn't prepare me for this. The lights were right in my eyes, and more people crowded around me when they realized I was Conway's woman.

He pressed the microphone farther toward me. "Do you love Conway Barsetti?"

It was such a personal question, something I hadn't even said to him. But it was obvious to anyone who saw us together. Vanessa had just asked me when I knew he was the one, even though I'd never told her I loved him. The whole world believed we were in love, because that was exactly what they saw.

I didn't see the harm in saying it. It was long overdue, and I was exhausted from holding it in for so long. Like a secret I wanted to get off my chest, I let the truth fly from my lips. "Yes. Yes, I do."

11
CONWAY

I didn't realize Muse had called me until past midnight. The conversation with my family lasted longer than I anticipated. It ended on a cold note, just as cold as it was before. Instead of moving past this difficult time, we seemed to be in the exact same place.

I stayed at the hotel again that night because I didn't want to be at the house.

Even though I wasn't certain if I was welcome anyway.

I promised I wouldn't be involved in the Underground anymore, and it was a promise I'd never wanted to make. I was furious my father didn't admire me even a little bit for what I did. I spent thirty million of my own money to save a girl I didn't even know.

Still didn't know her name.

And that meant nothing to him?

I understood my father just wanted to protect me. I wasn't that dense. But he obviously didn't respect me as a grown man. Most of the time, he acted like he did. But once the circumstances changed, the truth came out.

I was too pissed to call Muse back. I would just be shitty company and probably piss her off. She was the only thing in my life that made me feel good, and I wasn't going to fuck that up by calling her right now. If she called again, I would answer. But I wasn't going to ruin her night by calling her.

The next day, Carter and I got into the SUV and drove back to my parents' house. The two of us didn't talk much last night, both too exhausted by all the bullshit we'd listened to all evening. There was nothing left to say anyway.

Carter was behind the wheel, his eyes full of exhaustion like he hadn't slept much the night before. "I'm gonna head back to Milan today."

"Good idea. There's nothing left to do here anyway."

He faced forward again, one hand on the wheel as he drove through the countryside. He drove a Range Rover, even though it wasn't related to the cars he designed for his company. "How'd you sleep?"

"I didn't sleep."

"Me neither," he said. "I thought we'd be past this by now, but they still seem pissed at us."

"I know... It's like we're children."

"Ridiculous, right?"

Fifteen minutes later, we pulled up to the house and walked inside. My mother greeted us by the door, and despite the heavy conversation we'd had the night before, she hugged me tightly and kissed me on the cheek. I felt her love surround me, unconditional and everlasting.

I was grateful I always had her love—no matter what. Not everyone could say the same thing about their mothers.

She hugged Carter the same way, showering him with love like he was her son too.

"We just wanted to say goodbye," I said. "Carter and I are heading back home. We've got work to do." A part of me wanted to leave without saying goodbye to my father. I didn't want to see him, and I suspected he didn't want to see me either.

"I understand," Mom said. "I'll be right back."

Carter and I stood together in the entryway, waiting for this all to end so we could get back to our lives.

Uncle Cane came first and walked with Carter outside for privacy. Maybe he was going to scold his son and didn't want me to overhear it. I was about to have the same conversation with my father, so I didn't see why it mattered.

My father arrived a few minutes later but without my

mother. He slowly walked toward me, wearing black jeans and a black t-shirt. He would normally be at the winery right now, but work seemed to be put on hold in light of everything that had happened.

He didn't look at me as he approached, his powerful arms hanging by his sides. His gaze was indecipherable, but his mood was loud as a bell. Still disappointed and still ticked, he was exactly the same as he was yesterday...and the day before.

He stopped in front of me and crossed his arms over his chest. He finally looked at me, his dark eyes like bullets.

I held his gaze, refusing to be intimidated—even by my father. "I'm heading back to work. Just wanted to say goodbye."

Silence.

I was usually on my father's good side, so I wasn't used to this kind of shunning. It made me realize that no one wanted to be my father's enemy. Even without a gun, he was terrifying. How did my mom, so full of warmth and affection, put up with him?

It didn't seem like he was going to say anything, so I wasn't going to wait around. "I guess I'll talk to you later, then." I turned away, finished with his coldness.

"Con." Like a blade, his word sliced through the air.

I stopped mid-turn, then slowly came back to him.

"There's a lot you don't know about me, son. And I kept it that way for a reason."

I stared into his eyes, waiting for him to elaborate.

"I've changed my life and have become a good man. I've done a lot of things I'm not proud of. When I was your age, I was reckless and stupid because I had nothing to lose. I didn't have a wife or children. And I had the ridiculous notion that I was invincible. It's hard to believe I'm standing here today, a healthy man with a beautiful family."

"If you've done terrible things, how can you stand there and judge me?"

"I've never judged you, Con."

"Seems like it."

"I just don't want you to make the mistakes that I've made. You are..." His voice trailed off, and he took a deep breath. He stared at the ground before he lifted his gaze to meet mine once again. "There are no words to describe how I feel about you...my only son. I love you more than myself. I even love you more than your mother, as unbelievable as that is. I'm only hard on you because I love you. You may be a grown man, but I'm never going to stop protecting you."

My anger dimmed slightly, but only a fraction. "I saved that woman. How can you not be proud of me?"

He sighed. "She's not your responsibility to save,

Conway. You have an illustrious career and a woman who loves you. Just live your life and be happy."

"You never answered the question."

His eyes narrowed, accompanied by a sigh. "You have no idea how proud I am of you. But I'm proud of you no matter what you do. I've always wanted you to take over the winery, but I knew you had your own ambitions. Not only did I respect it, but I supported them. But this...I do not...cannot support. Don't get involved with these people. It's not worth it."

I bowed my head slightly. "What kind of man did you used to be?" When the silence stretched, I wondered if he would answer. I knew bits and pieces about his past, but not a lot. I lifted my gaze to look at him again.

His expression was just as hard. "When I was young, all I cared about was money. My father was an arms dealer, and naturally, Cane and I inherited it. The blood war raged, and we made a lot of money selling weapons to all kinds of people. I've murdered men because they made the mistake of getting in my way. I didn't care if they had a wife or children. I didn't care about anything. I was cruel. Evil."

It was hard to imagine my father being anything other than the upstanding man he was today. All he seemed to care about was family, wine, and the beauty of Tuscany. "When did that all change?"

"Your mother."

"She didn't want you to be that man anymore?"

"No... I didn't want to be that man anymore. I wanted to deserve her. I wanted to protect her. You can't protect a woman if people constantly want your head on a spike. If anything, you're often the very reason she's in danger in the first place. I wanted a quiet life where we could raise a family and live in peace. I craved silence when all I ever wanted was war. When your mother told me she was pregnant with you, I knew I had to end all my wars. I had to change everything if I was going to bring you into this world. So, I sent her away to a safe place, and I fought until everything was finally said and done. I won't get into the specifics because they don't matter anymore. I can't start that up again. I can't kick the dust back into the air. I can't watch my son become involved in a life I've worked so hard to protect him from."

My father used to be a criminal and a murderer. I was nothing like that. "You're comparing me to yourself, but I've never killed anyone. All I've done is pulled women from the Underground."

"But that's where it starts, Con. And if they raise a gun to you, you have no other choice but to fight back. And you have to pull that trigger quicker than they do. Before you know it, you've started a war that will last a decade. I'm trying to save you time and heartache. You have a beautiful woman living in that house with you. If you don't care about yourself, at least care about her."

All I ever did was take care of her. I shielded her from everything that could possibly hurt her. It was practically my purpose.

"You promised you wouldn't go back there," my father said. "And Barsettis keep their promises."

"I know."

"Let this go. Forget about Bones. Forget about those women. You may save one woman, but that won't stop another hundred from being captured. When you cut off the head of a snake, two more will grow back."

"So we do nothing?" I asked quietly. "Just give up?"

His gaze turned cold again. "I've paid my dues, Conway. I've righted my wrongs. Let someone else deal with it now. The Barsettis have suffered far too long. It's our time to enjoy peace. If you have any respect for me and your mother, you will let us live the rest of our lives in peace. If you really need to do this, please wait until we're dead and gone."

Imagining them buried six feet under sent a wave of depression throughout my body. It made me weak, sick, and broken all at the same time. I was still resentful toward my father for being so harsh, but I couldn't refuse his request. I wouldn't take away his peace, not when it meant so much to him. He did an amazing job raising me. The least I could do in return was give him what he wanted. "I'll drop it, Father."

He closed his eyes for a brief moment. "Good."

I could never tell him the truth about my relationship with Muse. If I did, what would he think of me then? I bought her at the Underground and made her my prisoner. I took advantage of her because she was so weak. He would probably be even more disappointed in me.

Our relationship was different now, but it didn't change how it started. Maybe I cared about her now, maybe I would do anything to protect her now, but it wasn't always that way. "I should get going..."

"Yeah. You have a long drive ahead of you."

We faced each other in silence, neither one of us making the first move.

We were both stubborn like that.

But I was less stubborn. I moved in and hugged him.

He hugged me back. His arms remained around my body for a long time, and he held me close. He'd never held me this long, not since I was a boy.

I let the touch linger. I was a grown man with a billion-dollar empire, but at the end of the day, I was still a son who needed his father.

He pulled away and gripped both of my shoulders. "I love you, son."

"I love you too, Father."

He grabbed the back of my head and kissed me on the forehead. "Tell Sapphire your mother and I say hello."

I nodded. "I will." Turning away, I walked out of the house. I didn't want to look at my father again before leaving because it was too hard. He was always sad when I left. He did his best to hide it, but I could see it in his eyes.

Uncle Cane was gone, and Carter was leaning against the SUV while he waited for me. He was on his phone, the corner of his mouth raised in a smile.

"I guess your conversation went over well," I said as I walked to the vehicle.

He looked up from his phone, his eyes playful. "Yeah, we had our usual father-son talk. He's still a little pissed at me, but he'll get over it in time."

"Then why are you grinning like that?"

"Funny that you ask..." He clicked something on his screen then turned the phone around so I could see it.

The video showed Muse outside a restaurant. Vanessa was in the background, and some of the guys on my security team were escorting Muse to the car while the paparazzi pushed a camera into her face. First, they asked if she was living with me, which she never really answered.

I took the phone from him and watched the video with narrowed eyes. When did this video take place? Did she go out last night? Is that why she called me?

"Sapphire, do you love Conway Barsetti?" They

pushed the microphone at her and followed her as she headed to the car.

Instead of ignoring them again, a slight smile appeared on her lips. It was the same look she gave me when we sat across from each other during our intimate meals. It was the same look she gave me when she told me she missed me. It was real, not a mask she plastered on for the cameras.

And then she answered. "Yes. Yes, I do."

CARTER KEPT GLANCING AT ME FROM HIS SIDE OF THE car. We were slowly approaching Verona, just thirty minutes outside the city. "Con, we haven't said more than a few words to each other this whole drive. What's the deal?"

I wasn't in the mood to talk. That video kept flashing across my eyes over and over. I heard her voice as she said those simple words.

She loved me.

I knew it wasn't a publicity stunt. I saw the sincerity in her eyes. The fact that I didn't question it told me I had already suspected it anyway. It was obvious in her affection, the way she worried about me anytime I was gone. She slept on my chest every single night, and the second I wasn't there, her senses picked up on it. When I gave her freedom to leave, she chose to stay.

Now I knew why.

Carter whistled. "You alive over there?"

"Shut up, Carter." I stared out the window, unsure what I would do once I got back to the house. For a brief second, I'd felt warmth flood through my veins when I heard her declare her love for me. But then it turned ice-cold immediately afterward.

I told her I didn't want romance.

Or love.

I wasn't naïve enough to pretend she and I didn't have a deep relationship. We had friendship, trust, and loyalty to one another. If she really meant nothing to me, I'd have been fucking other women this entire time.

But she was all I wanted.

But that didn't mean I loved her.

Hardly.

Maybe she was arrogant enough to think I would change my mind. Maybe she thought I didn't know what I wanted. Maybe she mistook my affection for commitment.

I enjoyed what we had, but I didn't want forever.

I never wanted forever.

All things in life were temporary. Muse and I were no different. She ignited a fiery passion inside me, making me obsessed and protective. But that was an example of intense love, nothing more. This was just a phase, an inspiration for my career. But Muse wouldn't be my muse forever. Eventually, she would lose her allure, and I'd want someone else to replace her.

Even though that made me a dick, it was the truth.

Carter broke the silence again. "What is the big deal, Con? A beautiful woman loves you... Poor you. She's got to be the most gorgeous woman in the world right now. Everyone is obsessed with her—but she loves you."

"I don't want her to love me, Carter."

"Bullshit," he said. "You're so sprung off her."

"Yes, I know," I said quietly. "I'm obsessed with her. I care about her. But that's where it stops. I told her I didn't want anything more than that. I told her marriage and love would never be on the table...but she didn't believe me."

"And I don't blame her. No one would. You two act like—"

"Our relationship is intense, but it has a time limit."

"Why?" he asked. "Why does it have to have an expiration date?"

"Because that's not how I design lingerie. Lingerie is about passion. Monogamy already leads to stale and boring relationships. I can't have that."

"You've already proven you're the best of the best, Conway. I think you can take a step back and cruise."

"I don't want to cruise," I argued.

"And it seems like our parents are still in love," he pointed out. "So, your theory about staleness is incorrect."

I finally looked at him. "If it's incorrect, then why haven't you ever had a woman for more than a night."

He held my look in return. "Because I haven't found my muse."

I looked away again, seeing Verona come into view.

He turned onto the road and approached my house. The gates were opened, and he drove into the roundabout. He put the vehicle in park but didn't get out. "Con."

I'd already opened the door. "What?"

"Women like her don't come around often. Your family loves her, and she puts up with your bullshit. So, don't do anything stupid, alright?"

I felt my jaw clench before I shut the door.

The men carried my stuff inside, and I walked into the house. The muscles of my torso immediately clenched once I was in my own home—because I knew I was about to look at her. There was so much anger inside me, resentment toward my parents and fury toward her.

Why did she have to say that?

Why couldn't she have just left it alone?

We were happy. Our relationship was perfect, in its own twisted way. But now it was destroyed because she took it to a new level.

She could have just walked away from those reporters.

Or better yet, she could have stayed home like I asked her to.

I reached the third floor, my arms shaking because they were so tense. The veins in my arms were thicker than usual, blood circulating at a high velocity. My temper had been ignited, and I tried my best to put it out with an attempt at calmness.

I stepped inside my bedroom and found her sitting on the couch, watching TV in just my t-shirt. She'd already showered after work, but she didn't put makeup on her face. She jumped slightly when the door swung open, clearly not expecting me. "Con, you scared the shit out of me."

Con. It was a nickname only my family used. I'd liked it when she used it the first time, but now I recognized it as a sign of her possessiveness over me. She felt like she owned me, had a piece of me.

But I was the one who owned her.

She got off the couch and walked up to me in the doorway. She ignored my look of ferocity and moved into my chest, her arms wrapping around me. She rested her head on my chest and released a deep sigh. "I missed you..."

I was still angry, but when I smelled her hair and felt her affection, it was difficult to keep my feelings of rage. Like a queen, she commanded my emotions and brought me to a simmer. She sucked the anger right out of my skin, absorbing it like a sponge.

My arms moved around her.

"I'm glad you're home. I couldn't handle this separation any longer."

I'd planned on telling her off the second I walked through the door. I wanted to scream at her for leaving the property while I was gone, even if she had my security team with her. I wanted to tell her that saying she loved me to a camera was the dumbest decision she'd ever made.

But I didn't. I rested my chin on her head and felt her softness.

"I didn't sleep well. It's not the same without you here." Her hands migrated underneath my shirt and glided up my chest, feeling the muscles of my stomach. She moved to my sternum, her fingertips lightly touching me. "And I miss having this…" She glided her hand over my chest and down my stomach. Her fingers felt the top of my pants, and she yanked on the top button to make it come loose. "I miss having you between my legs."

I closed my eyes and felt my cock come to life. I was livid just moments before, and now I was soft and hard at the same time. The second this beautiful woman touched me and told me how much she missed me, all my rage disappeared. All I could think about was how good her hands felt on my body, how hard my dick got when she told me she missed fucking me for the past few days. She was just in my t-shirt, her panties acting as her bottoms.

She finally tilted her head upward to look at me, her hand wrapped around my length and stroking him. "Make love to me." She rose on her tiptoes and kissed me.

I tried not to kiss her back, tried to fight the goodness that flooded my body. But the second those soft lips were on mine, I couldn't fight it. I kissed her deeply, giving her my tongue when I felt hers. My cock twitched in her hand because these past three days had been as difficult for him as it was for her.

My hands moved into her hair, and I kissed her harder, passion overriding the rage. With every shared embrace, our current situation seemed to fade away. I wasn't thinking about anything anymore. Now all I wanted was her, to fall into the throes of passion that she gave me.

I guided her back to the bed, clothes coming off as we went. I got her on the bed, moved between her legs, and finally slid my cock inside her.

And then I was gone.

I LEFT EARLY THE NEXT MORNING AND DROVE to Milan.

I walked into my studio and sat there with a cup of

coffee, staring at my sketchbook blankly, the pencil sitting on the paper. It was overcast that day, the first hint of fall reaching us. The days of brutal heat and humidity would start to dwindle, and as we moved into the fall, snow would arrive.

I drank my coffee and spun the pencil in my fingertips, having no inspiration whatsoever.

I was too pissed.

I fucked Muse last night—twice in a row. Then we lay in silence together before drifting off to sleep. We didn't speak to each other. I didn't dig into her for all the mistakes she'd made.

I stayed awake for a long time, staring at the ceiling and feeling her cuddled next to my side. I wanted to push her off me, but I also wanted to pull her closer. Two versions of myself existed, one that wanted to pack her bags and kick her out of my house, and another that wanted to keep burying myself between her legs every night.

Who would win?

Now, I sat there in my studio, silence surrounding me like a constant drum in the background. All the models were on vacation, visiting their families wherever they were from. Orders continued to pile in, and the media worshiped the designs I created. Now that Muse had told the world she loved me, I wondered if it changed the outcome of all my hard work.

Nicole walked inside, her clipboard tucked into the crook of her arm. "What are you doing here, Conway?"

"I own this building." I didn't need to give anyone an explanation.

Nicole brushed off my coldness. "I thought you were taking some time off."

"I did. Now I'm ready to work again."

Nicole came around the table and looked down at my blank sketch pad. Her eyes shifted back to me, full of accusation. "Doesn't seem that way."

No one spoke to me that way, but Nicole could get away with it—because she knew I'd be devastated if she ever left Barsetti Lingerie.

"Something on your mind?"

One thing. "No."

Even though she knew I was lying, she didn't push it. "How was Greece?"

Fucking perfect. I spent my afternoons sailing with Muse or exploring the small town. Our nights were spent fucking in the pool. The trip was short, but it was exactly what I wanted. But now I looked back on the memory with resentment. "Good."

She set the clipboard on the table and looked through the papers. "I'm sure you're aware that Sapphire made a very public declaration the other night. Not sure if it was staged or not, but the world loved it. Orders increased by an additional twenty-five percent."

I slowly turned to her, wearing an incredulous look. "You're fucking kidding me."

"No."

I slowly dragged my hands through my hair and down my face.

Nicole stood beside me in silence, giving me a moment to recover. "Isn't that a good thing, Conway?"

"A good thing that this woman has this much power over me?" I snapped. "No, it's not a good fucking thing." I tossed my sketchbook off the table and onto the floor. The pencil rolled away then clanked when it hit the hardwood floor.

Nicole didn't flinch, used to my violent outbursts. "She's had this much power over you since the first day she walked in here. And she's had the same power over the entire world."

12
SAPPHIRE

Conway was gone when I woke up the next morning. Since we'd been apart for days, I didn't expect him to run off without saying two words to me. I called him, but he didn't answer. And after five hours had passed, he still hadn't called me back.

He was quiet when he got home yesterday, but I just assumed spending time with his family had taken a toll on him. They weren't getting together for dinner and a celebration. They were preparing for a potential war. Tensions were high.

So, I gave him his space.

But I was hurt that he left for the entire day—and didn't even call me back.

I worked in the stables all day then took a shower. The

sun had been blocked by the clouds, so it wasn't as warm as usual. It was a nice respite, but I still preferred the hot sun over a blanket of clouds.

When I got out of the shower, Conway finally walked through the door.

I sighed in relief when I saw his muscular build in a formfitting t-shirt. If he hadn't returned in the next hour, I would have called him again. And if he didn't answer, I wouldn't have stopped calling until he picked up.

I didn't ask him where he'd been or why he didn't call me back. I decided to just leave it alone. "Hey."

All I got was a look.

I ran my fingers through my hair, then moved in to him to kiss him. I rose on my tiptoes and kissed his mouth, feeling the stubble from his chin. He hadn't shaved in the past few days, so his chin was coarser than it usually was. I kissed him, but his embrace wasn't particularly affectionate. "Long day?" I asked.

"Something like that." He stepped away from me the second I let go, like he couldn't get away from me fast enough.

It stung. "You want to have dinner in here? Or on the terrace?"

"I already ate." He opened the drawer to his dresser and pulled out workout clothes.

I couldn't remember a time when we didn't eat together, except when I first came to live with him. Once our relationship had changed, we shared all our meals at the same time, especially dinner. "Conway, what's wrong?"

"Nothing." He grabbed his headphones and changed into his shorts and a fresh t-shirt. "I'm just not hungry."

I wanted to be patient with him, but now I wasn't buying these lies. "Conway."

He left his jeans on the floor and dropped his phone into his pocket. Like I hadn't said his name at all, he kept going.

"What happened with your family?"

"Nothing that concerns you."

My eyebrows almost shot off my face in shock. He gave me a backhand without actually touching me. "Why are you being such an ass?"

He finally looked at me, his gaze ice-cold. "Because I'm an ass. I've always been an ass, and I'll always be an ass. I'm a fucking asshole that only wants good sex and peace and quiet. It's not my fault that you ever expected me to be anything more than what I am." He shoved his earphones into his canals and stormed off.

I was in such shock that I didn't stop him. I watched him walk away, watched this man I hardly knew leave the bedroom. He looked like Conway and sounded like Conway...but he wasn't the man that I knew. Something had set him off, and now he wasn't a person I recognized.

Even at our worst, he'd never spoken to me that way.

He'd never treated me that way.

Conway never came back. He went on his run and disappeared.

I had dinner alone in the bedroom and waited for him like a wife waiting for her cheating husband to walk through the door.

But he never came.

If he was on the property, there was only one place he would be. His studio was his safe zone, the place where he produced beautiful pieces he was proud of. It was late, so he would normally be in bed right now, but if he wasn't in the bedroom with me, that's where he would be.

Unless he went out instead.

The door was shut, but light escaped through the crack underneath. Dante would never leave that light on by accident, so I knew it was occupied. I opened the door and let myself inside. Just as I expected, he was sitting at the table with his sketchbook in front of him.

He didn't look up.

I slowly approached the table, examining the sweat lines on his t-shirt. He'd worked out hard but didn't shower afterward. That was unlike him. Standing beside him, I waited for something to happen.

He kept sketching, making a simple black corset that wasn't memorable.

"Conway."

His hand stilled, but he still didn't look at me.

"Talk to me."

He finally set the pencil down and looked at me, but his fierce expression showed his rage. "What, Sapphire? What do you want to talk about?"

Like he'd backhanded me again, I was nearly knocked off my feet. He could say the coldest things to me, but nothing was more insulting than calling me by my first name. He hadn't done that since he'd first learned it. I hardly identified with the name anymore. Muse was my name now. It was my identity.

And he took it away.

"Don't call me that," I whispered.

He wasn't the same handsome man he used to be. Now he looked different, hostile. "It's your name."

"Muse is my name."

He held my gaze, his shoulders rigid and hard. His

body was tighter than usual, like he was ready for a fight to break out. He was strung tighter than I'd ever seen him, as though he could snap like a rubber band if he were stretched any further. "What do you want? I'm working."

"What do I want?" I asked in shock. "I want you to stop being an ass and just tell me what's wrong."

"Nothing is wrong," he snapped. "I don't have to spend every waking minute with you if I don't want to. You aren't the center of my world, Sapphire. You aren't—"

I slapped him across the face. "Don't call me that."

He turned with the hit, his jaw clenched tight. He slowly turned away, his face turning red from ferocity, not from the mark I'd just landed on his face. His body tightened even more, but he didn't rise out of his chair. "Get. The. Fuck. Out."

I lost my temper when I hit him, and now that the dialogue was coming to an end, I knew I didn't accomplish what I set out to do. "Conway, you leave for a few days, and you come back as a whole different person. What the hell happened?"

He slowly rose to his feet, his arms shaking as the adrenaline pumped through his veins. "Get. Out."

This time, I actually feared him. I was afraid of the way he stared at me, afraid of the way he leered over me with his size and strength. His arms shook, like he was barely controlling himself from grabbing me by the neck.

I didn't feel comfortable there.

Just like I had been with Knuckles, I was afraid.

I was actually afraid.

HE DIDN'T COME TO THE BEDROOM THAT NIGHT, AND I knew he wasn't going to.

I still didn't understand what had happened.

It was like he hated me.

His cold treatment was unbearable, but it was nothing compared to the unknown. I had no idea what was causing him to behave this way. Even a fight with his father wouldn't make him snap like this. When I spoke to him in his hotel room, he was upset about the way things were going...but he never shut me out.

I didn't know what to do, so I decided to ask the one person who would.

Carter.

I sent a text to Vanessa. *Can you give me Carter's number?*

She sent the number immediately, along with a happy face.

It was ironic because nothing about this was happy. I called the number and listened to it ring.

Carter answered with a deep voice that was similar to Conway's. "Carter."

"Hey, it's Sapphire." My voice was beginning to crack before I even started the conversation. "I'm sorry to bother you, but…"

"Fuck, what did he do?" he asked with a sigh.

"Ever since he came home, he's been a completely different person. He's cold, mean… Not the man I know. He won't talk to me, and he can barely stand to be in the same room with me. But he won't tell me what happened. I know this isn't your problem, but could you tell me what's going on? Do you know anything? Did something happen?"

"Jesus," he said with another sigh. "Conway is fucking stupid. That's what's going on."

I waited for a more detailed response.

"I showed him that video where you said you loved him…"

They shoved a microphone in my face, and I'd just admitted the truth. The weight had been taken off my shoulders, and I actually felt good about it. I didn't care whether Conway saw it or not, but I assumed he wouldn't. He didn't strike me as a man who watched the news about himself. "So? Why would that matter? I know he loves me too." He didn't strike me as a petty man who would get upset that I told the whole world first before saying it to him in private.

"Uh..." Carter paused as he tried to find the right words to say. "According to him, that's not how he feels."

Slowly, my heart started to sink into my stomach. I felt it grow smaller, all my joy and love disappearing. I wasn't ashamed to wear my heart on my sleeve and love Conway openly, despite our difficult beginning, and that made this blow so much harder to take. "He said he didn't love me..."

Carter didn't say anything.

"That's what he said?" I pressed.

"I don't know. That's what he says, but I think he's lying to himself. I've seen the way he is with you, and I know he's happy."

"But that doesn't matter to him."

"He wants everything to stay the same. He just wants you to be a man and a woman. He says he doesn't want marriage or love, because that stuff fades, and then the passion goes stale and you're just stuck with someone you don't want to be stuck with..."

I closed my eyes and felt two tears escape. Our intense relationship had been reduced to nothing more than an inconvenience. He didn't think our passion would last forever because it was just lust, not love.

"Sapphire?"

I swallowed my tears and kept my voice steady. "Even so, that doesn't give him the right to treat me this way."

"I agree," he said. "Like I said, I don't think he means it. I think he's just struggling to accept the inevitable."

"Which is?"

"That he does love you…but he doesn't want to."

Another tear escaped, and I felt lower than I ever had. When I was running from Knuckles, I was scared, but I wasn't heartbroken. Ever since Conway had become part of my life, I'd been a happy person. He gave me a home, a place where I belonged. We had such a connection, such emotion.

How could he throw it all away?

"Thank you for telling me, Carter."

"Of course," he whispered. "You're a good person, Sapphire. Don't settle for a man who doesn't deserve you. I love my cousin like a brother, but he's got his head shoved up his ass right now."

Like all the other Barsettis, Carter was a good person. He was masculine and strong, but he showed affection when it mattered. Talking to me was a betrayal, but he knew it was the right thing to do. "I should go."

"Talk to him," he said. "You're the only person who can talk sense into him. I've already tried."

I used to have a strong effect on him, but that seemed like ancient history now. "I will."

"Bye."

"Bye." It was a relief to hang up, so I could let a few more tears fall in privacy. It was stupid to cry over a man, but Conway wasn't just any man. He was the man who owned my heart. When he let me go, he released his hold over my body, but I left my heart freely behind.

I wanted him to have it.

I wanted him to have all of me.

I wiped my tears away and allowed myself a few minutes to compose myself. I didn't want him to notice the evidence of my tears, the puffiness of my face and the redness in my eyes. I controlled my emotions long enough for them to die away before I went in search of him.

My heart was beating so fast.

I didn't know how this conversation was going to go, but I suspected it wouldn't go well. But I hoped I could say the right things to calm him down.

There were dozens of bedrooms in this place, and I didn't want to search one by one. Knowing him, he wasn't sleeping.

He was drinking.

I went to his office, even though he almost never used it. I opened the door and found him sitting behind the desk, smoking a cigar and drinking scotch right out of the bottle. The smoke rose from his nostrils and drifted to the ceiling. His eyes were lidded, but he still wore the same malicious expression.

I refused to be afraid of him.

I walked across the room and stopped in front of his desk. I'd asked him to stop smoking, but my wishes obviously meant nothing to him. If he wanted to smoke and die, fine. I wouldn't waste any more time trying to stop him. "You're a coward." I planted my hands against the desk and stared him down.

His eyes immediately narrowed at my words.

"You're a coward for many reasons. Number one, you come home acting like the biggest dick face in the world. You treat me like garbage, and you don't have the balls to tell me what your problem is. Instead, you ignore me until I confront you about it. Number two, you're pissed that I had the strength to tell the whole world that I love you, and you're too scared to admit it yourself."

He lowered his cigar, his eyes contracting farther.

"You can sit there and say you don't feel the same way, but that's a bunch of bullshit. You're in love with me, it's obvious in everything that you do. It's obvious in the way you tell me you miss me, obvious in the way you need me. You kiss me like I'm the only woman who's ever meant anything to you—because I am. I'm sorry this didn't go the way you wanted, but you're going to have to get over it. You're lucky I'm still here at all."

He sucked on his cigar again, his eyes unblinking.

I gripped the edge of the desk between my forefingers and thumb, feeling the sweat from my palms coat the smooth wood.

"Man up, Conway. First, apologize. Then tell me you love me."

He released the smoke from his lips, his eyes trained on my face. His expression was carefully controlled, his thoughts hidden deep within his eyes. He was calmer than earlier, but it was probably just an act. His hostility was still evident, obvious in the rigid way he held himself.

He dropped the cigar directly on the desk and slowly rose to his feet. He planted both of his hands against the desk and gave me a ferocious stare. "Sapphire." All he did was say my name, and that told me how the rest of this was going to go. "I told you this relationship meant nothing. You're just some woman I fuck. You're just some woman who occupies my time. I don't love you now, nor will I ever. Marriage and romance were never on the table. It's not my fault you thought otherwise."

I kept up my glare, refusing to show just how much those words hurt. I refused to cry, to allow him to witness my heart breaking in real time.

"You crossed a line when you told those reporters how you felt about me. You told the world something they never should have heard. You brought my personal life into the limelight. You had no right to do that."

"And I would do it again," I said coldly. "Because I meant it, Conway."

"And I wish you didn't." He let go of the desk and stood upright.

"Is that really all you care about?" I asked incredulously. "Work? Conway, there's more to life than being the best at something. There's more to life than money. Has your own family taught you nothing?"

"Don't talk about my family," he snapped. "They're mine, not yours."

That hurt as much as anything else he'd said. I'd developed a deep affection for his family, felt like they were my own. I'd never had a sister, and I'd never had parents who were so attentive and loving.

"And yes, work is the most important thing to me. It's my identity, my legacy."

"A legacy should be family, Conway. You should have a wife and children, people who will remember you when you're gone—and not the money that you made. I've never cared about your success or your wealth. I fell in love with the man underneath the suit, all the good and the bad."

"And I never asked you to."

I was talking to a monster, a heartless monster. He wasn't even Conway anymore. "If you really didn't feel the same way in return, I would accept that. Because that's not what love is about. It's given freely without expecting anything in return. But to treat me this way...is disgusting. You're lucky I'm still standing here."

"Or seriously unlucky."

The insults kept piling on, but with every new one, the bruise turned an even darker shade of purple. He was stabbing me with a knife, sinking the blade in deeper and deeper. He would keep going until I couldn't handle it anymore. "I feel sorry for you for being that afraid of love."

He remained focused, and his expression didn't change.

"The thing you're most afraid of is your parents' disappointment. Well, they'd be seriously disappointed in you right now." I turned away from his desk, prepared to retreat to my room and sob until my eyes were swollen shut.

"Get out."

"I'm going, asshole."

"No. Get the fuck out of my house."

I turned around to see the new look of rage on his face. Now he was no longer silently calm. His face was tinted red, but not in a sexy way like when we were in bed together. He was furious, the vein in his forehead pulsing. He gripped the desk like he might flip it over and break down the window behind him.

He knew I didn't have a cent to my name. He knew I had nothing but clothes and shoes. I was completely dependent on him, and without him, I was nothing. But that didn't matter to him. Our beautiful relationship had been stripped away like it didn't matter in the first place.

Like I never mattered.

I refused to believe Conway was really this cruel. My last comment about his parents obviously pushed him further than he was prepared to go. But just the fact that he said it told me he wasn't afraid to cross all lines.

I'd never been so disappointed in him. "I'll be gone in fifteen minutes."

"Make it ten."

I GRABBED A BAG AND STUFFED IT WITH MY ESSENTIALS. I grabbed as many clothes as I could fit and one pair of shoes. I didn't have a lot of room, so I had to leave most of the things I loved behind.

I stared at his top drawer, the place where he kept his t-shirts. It was the stuff he usually wore around the house on a lazy Sunday. It was the first place I went for a comfy shirt to wear to bed. Because the cotton smelled like him. Because the fabric reminded me of him. I slept in his shirt every single night while he was away because that was as close as I could get to him.

I wasted thirty seconds staring at that drawer when I should have been hauling ass.

But then I made my decision.

I yanked it open and took a handful of his t-shirts. I had to ditch one of my favorite dresses in order to make them fit in the bag, but I didn't care. I left the dress on the floor in front of the dresser and finally walked out.

I wanted to be proud and pretend I didn't need his clothes, but I knew once I was alone, I would regret not having them. I didn't have a picture of him or anything else to remember our time. All I had was his scent, his touch.

So, I swallowed my pride and walked out.

I headed to the entryway, where some of the men were waiting for me.

Conway was nowhere in sight.

A man in a leather jacket handed me a set of keys. "He said you can keep it."

I stepped out to see a bright red Ferrari waiting for me. I didn't want any of his things, but I needed a getaway car right now. I would return it the second I could.

"And Mr. Barsetti wants you to have this as well." He held up a black suitcase.

I didn't need to look inside to know what was there.

Cash.

I grabbed the briefcase from his hand and tossed it across the roundabout and onto the lawn. It landed with a heavy thud and snapped open, all the bills flying out across the grass. "Tell Mr. Barsetti I don't want his money—I was never his whore."

I got into the two-seater speedster and set my bag on the passenger seat. Thankfully, the cars were the same as they were in the US, and they drove on the same sides of the road. The engine was packed with immaculate horsepower, and I had no experience driving such a beast.

But I could pretend that I did.

I hit the gas hard and sped off, the engine roaring to life as I sped into the darkness and away from the house. I kept up a brave face even though no one could see me. I wanted my last moment on his property to be a proud one. I would hold my head high. I would keep a perfect posture. I would be unafraid.

Just like I was on the runway.

But once I was a few miles away, the sadness kicked in.

And I started to cry.

I grabbed my phone from my bag and called the first person who came to mind. It was the only opportunity that I had, and now that I was on my own, I had to be resourceful. Conway wouldn't take care of me anymore, and I had to take care of myself. I did it before him—and I could do it after him.

Andrew Lexington picked up. "Sapphire, I have to be honest and say I wasn't expecting you to call."

That makes two of us. "I apologize for calling so late, but I was wondering if the offer was still on the table?" I stopped my tears from escaping over the line. No one liked the sound of desperation.

Andrew didn't say anything for a long time, but I could feel his smile over the phone. "For a woman like you, it's always on the table."

ALSO BY PENELOPE SKY

Muse told the world how she felt about me.

Instead of feeling joy, I felt terror.

This isn't what I want.

This isn't how our relationship is supposed to be.

I end things because I have no other choice.

But I struggle to cope with my misery, to sleep in an empty bed without her beside me.

Order Now

Printed in Great Britain
by Amazon